THE CURSE OF THE ANCIENT ARCHWAY

First Edition

Siona Rao

Chapters

1. The strange object 1
2. I make a phone call 6
3. Celebrations and deciphering 16
4. The curse 25
5. Secrets 31
6. Nephia's room 41
7. The strange man 57
8. The big reveal 68
9. TANTRUM 86
10. Goodbyes 93
11. On the plane 105
12. We land 109
13. Mira 113
14. Hawk! 116
15. An encounter in my bedroom 125
16. Death 130
17. The final battle 134
18. Welcome 144

EPILOGUE 148

1. The strange object

Look, I never wanted to be mixed up in all this strange, curse business and lead my friends into death traps.

I guess I should first introduce myself. I am Jadie Hills, and I live in a hotel with my mum, dad, and sister. It is located on Shady Lane, Picton Village, England. My parents work at the hotel, so we live in the annexe. My dad is the main chef while my mum is the Head of the hotel. My parents love history so we have a huge hall called the 'Museum', which is packed with stuff you would find in a real one. Nearly every week a new object presents itself to us. I have slowly taken liking to these strange mysterious objects. I am 11 years old. My hair is black, the same as my mum's. She is Indian. She grew up in Bangalore, India. Her name is Julie. My dad's name is Paul. He likes to wear winter clothes all year round because he always gets cold. Now, he is wearing a scarf, hat and mittens while the sun is glaring outside. I'm dressed in blue shorts and a magenta shirt. I am still feeling hot. I also have a sister Lucy. She is older than me and loves her phone.

I was looking at some strange items in the museum when something caught my eye. In front of the glass window, I saw something hurtling fast towards Earth. My heart plummeted as my eyes saw a heavy slab of stone crashing into the shed. Bits of splinter flew everywhere. All the contents of the shed were now hardly visible by the large amount of wood and dust covering it.

I ran to the kitchen to my dad. He was ladling a vast spoonful of vegetables and fish heads into a bubbling pot of stew. My tummy ignored the delicious smell as I raced to him.

"Hills, what on earth are you doing? Get back to room number 610!" snapped the manager of the hotel, who is called Mr Jacks, as he saw me racing towards my dad. My room number is 610 where we all live and where my sister is now, probably playing on her beloved phone. I ignored him.

"Dad! You must come! Mum's museum is in danger!" I cried, skidding to a halt and bashing my head on the oven door and trying to ignore the stitch in my side. My dad accidentally pulled the bag of salt into the stew while knocking the wine into the cake batter. He spilled the kettle water on the floor as he rushed off to the museum. The manager Mr Jacks looked alarmed as he put the cake batter in the oven, tasted the stew, and slipped on the water before singeing his head.

My dad quickly went to the shed, and I watched as I followed. I saw my father tending to the hole in the shed before stepping inside. I rushed outside to him and peeked into the shed.

The hotel is on Shady Lane, which might sound odd but the bright cheerful houses on the side of the road would make you think that this place is a jolly place, which it is. Or at least I thought it was. The thought of a random object crashing into my shed gave an air of mystery...

As my eyes adjusted to the darkness, I saw a huge slab of rock now covered in mud and dirt as it had landed on the shed. I looked at this giant rock wondering if something could be inside...

Ten minutes later, my dad and I had heaved the rock into the lift, much to the disapproval of Mr. Jacks, and took the elevator to number 999 of the hotel, which had a secret combination. My mum wasn't pleased to see us, especially when my dad's snow boots dropped mud on her immaculate carpet. She grieved the loss of the hole in the shed and the slight ash on the roof of the museum more than being interested in the strange object. She decided that it was too late to discuss the matter further (it was six o'clock) and that they would talk about it in the morning. We were asked to leave the rock in her office.

I was on my way down alone when my best friends Liam West, Jake White, and Mira Partail saw me coming down the marble staircase as they had just finished their dinner. Mira was a tall student who normally brought books with her. She was a fast runner and a pretty good swimmer. She had dark, long tresses and she was staying at the hotel because her mum was a cook, and her dad was a cleaner. She moved here from India 5 years ago.

Jake was the kind of boy who would never get satisfied with what he ate and would always want more. He loved sports and was good in running, swimming, basketball, football and pretty much everything else. He stayed at the hotel because his dad oversaw the sports activities and was a lifeguard at the swimming pool.
Liam was quite humorous and loved to draw sketches of what he saw, but it was normally his family and friends. He came here every summer holiday with his family, for 2 weeks.

"What are you doing?" cried Mira the second she saw me coming towards them. I quickly explained what I had seen, not pausing for Liam's hasty questions or Mira's gasps of fascination. I suddenly realised that I had not had my dinner yet and was now ravenous. I rushed up after saying bye to the three of them.

I dashed down the marble staircase and grabbed a sandwich from the bar. I scoffed it down in practically two seconds and took another one. It was not until my dad saw me that I reluctantly left for our room.

On the way, I met the horrible person who lived opposite us. She was called Ms Henrietta Smith. She was walking with Jessica Doves. Jessica was very sweet and cordial and was practically friends with everyone, but she didn't like to hang out with Mrs Smith for too long. I wondered why she even started walking with her in the first place.

"That cat! Its hair is so scruffy and unpleasant! I tried locking it in a spare cage I had to see if it did the trick but it escaped! Yesterday, I trod on his foot, but he can still walk!" I heard Mrs Smith complain to Jessica, who looked disgusted with the former's actions. The horrible woman was wearing the queerest garment. She was wearing a cloak like a witch but of course she couldn't be one! As she suddenly caught sight of me and swiftly turned away, her billowing grey cloak whacked me in the face with its ridiculous stitches. I don't know why she wears a stupid, witch-like cloak in the hotel. I was just about to pull the room door open, but the door suddenly swung towards me and whacked me hard in the face. I saw Lucy, my sister stroll carelessly back to the coffee table, her face practically a few millimetres away from her phone.

"Oi! You don't have to do that every time!" I cried angrily, sporting my smarting nose. She didn't reply as she was now laughing about something. I sat down. I thought about what had happened earlier this evening. I really wanted to know what was inside the rock, but I couldn't go into my mum's special office. Unless...

20 minutes later, I had dialled the secret code and was at my mum's office. I stepped back in the lift and dialled the number again, this time adding a five. The lift doors parted, and I saw that I was in the attic. I crept in. The only reason I knew this place was because I had seen my mum's manual. I decided to explore. Through the gloom, I could hardly see my own hands in front of me. I grabbed a candlestick and could just barely see through the darkness.

I know this sounds strange, but I don't know the hotel's original name. The reason is that, one day, a man came to the hotel and told my grandparents, who were the owners of the hotel then, to change the name. We started to call it Hotel Saturn as the man had suggested, but my mum had said that we should not utter the name (even though she didn't know why). Now, I think I just found out the original name.

2. I make a phone call

Hotel Srakolian.

The piece of precious, ancient parchment in front of me spelt out 2 words. I was certain that this was the name. I looked up and saw two brown, shining eyes blink in the darkness, causing me to utter a little scream. Mira hastily clamped her hand on my mouth.

"Mira! What are you doing?" I asked in alarm. She said she wanted to know more about the stone that I had mentioned earlier and had followed me here. She ignored *my* questions and pushed me aside gently. She stared at the parchment.

"Hotel Srakolian." she whispered. The candles in my hand flickered and grew menacingly till it was 3 feet tall and then disappeared. The light had vanished, and we were left in utter darkness. I looked puzzled as everything seemed to be flickering - every little object in this place. Then the light was extinguished, and cold air rushed in from the window. I could not see Mira who was only a few centimetres away from my face.

"Why did you say the blasted name?" I snapped at her.
"What...why...how..." she burbled, before realising the effects that the name had. I hoped dearly that she was not going to say the name again. I rummaged in my jersey pockets and found my special items.
- A torch
- A whistle
- A knife
- A rope
- A compass

- Walkie talkie pairs

I groped around for my torch and switched it on. Although the candlelight had shown a path for me, I did not see an open sarcophagus, a row of skulls on the floor and many strange and mysterious items. Mira and I tiptoed towards the end of the passage in the attic. Suddenly, we heard my dad and mum talking softly, in the floor below. It was then when I realised that the rock was a few metres ahead of us. My parents must have placed it up here in the attic, before they went into my mum's office, which was on the main floor. We waited till mum and dad left to our room 610. I shone the torch towards the crack. Then, we slowly and carefully lowered ourselves down the hole, forgetting for a split-second where we were landing on. I gave a small wince. We had landed on my mum's neatly stacked, important papers.

"Oh no! Your parents will get suspicious when they see your mum's papers all over the place!" Mira cried. I ignored her and took out my mum's landline, dialling my uncle's number. My uncle is an archaeologist and would probably love to help with this mystery. I wanted to invite him over, but I didn't want my parents to know that I had been the one to call him. So, I tried to confuse my parents and uncle. I waited for him to answer and after a few rings, he did.

He knew it was my mum's number and started to speak, "Hi Julie! Having a good summer? I heard that in your part of the country, it is like an oven in there! Mine has a nice moderate breeze. How is little Judie? And her big sister Lacy?" he asked. I tried to put on my mum's voice, but I failed considerably. "Hello Uncle Sa- sorry, Sam. I just thought that perhaps you could come round as we- "I began before he interrupted. "Judie? Is that you. No, it's Jodie, right?" Uncle Sam said. I sighed. He always forgets my name. He also forgets my sister's as well. I tried to block out Mira's giggles. "Can you come to the hotel and see this mysterious item that crashed here from outer space? And by the way my name is Judy, not Jadie or Jody." I said, thinking what my parents would say if he mentioned that I called him. I spoke to him for a few minutes and explained what I could. I'm not sure what he made of it. After the call finished, I turned to Mira who was quite pink and was laughing hard. I told her to meet me in the morning and with that, we left to our rooms.

Before I left, I took a biscuit from my mum's drawer, and washed it down with a glass of water. I dashed back down to my luxurious room and got a huge lecture from my dad about hoodlums and disappearances. I hardly understood the words, but I knew that I had been gone for too long.

Mira and I had everything planned for the next day, in case Uncle Sam showed up. Mira went to greet Uncle Sam disguised as me. I was hidden inside an old cupboard used for putting in the mops. Luckily, Uncle Sam was short sighted and gladly came inside. Mira cleverly disappeared. My parents stared at him and listened with puzzled faces while he explained that Judy had called him.

"Are you sure that it wasn't Jadie?" My mum asked anxiously, wincing as Uncle Sam squeezed her shoulders in greeting. I held my breath. "The young lady clearly stated that her name was Judy", the rather odd man declared. I watched from the crack in the door as I crossed my fingers. My parents looked highly suspicious but allowed Uncle Sam to look at the rock before they put it into the museum. They hurried off, as my dad needed to make curry for the day's dinner and my mum had to sort out why Mr. Jacks wouldn't step into the 5th corridor on the 2nd floor (probably because the swimming coach for our pool downstairs had left all the soap spilling onto the floor).

Mira 'happened' to be walking near our room and mum saw her. She asked Mira to accompany Uncle Sam to her office and leave him there. Mira took Uncle Sam there, and somehow managed to accompany him to the attic to look at the rock. I quickly ran out of the hiding place and followed their path, trying my best to hear what they were saying. I heard the clink of a hammer, the crumbling of rocks and Mira's gasps. Uncle Sam gasped and ran off to tell my parents something. As he left the room, Mira tiptoed to my second hiding place of that morning and whispered, "Come out: you must see this!" I did as she said and I saw that among a pile of rocks and rubble, a tall, grey statue stood, draped in a strange, vine-like material. I brushed away the vine-like stuff and saw a diamond shape inscribed on the figure. I looked in wonder while Mira moved restlessly by my side.

"Jadie, it is incredible!" she cried. I thought it was only fair that we should show Liam and Jake- after all they were our best friends. I knew my parents couldn't come to see the statue straightaway as they had plenty of work. We could bring it back later. We tried to lift the statue and it was surprisingly light. So, we heaved it to our secret den in the trees by the woods. It was only a minute away, but it felt rather long. I pushed the rock towards the corner and talked urgently into my walkie talkie. "Come right now, you must see what is in the den". In less than 2 minutes, Jake and Liam were huddled up in the den with us.

Liam was wearing a Hawaiian T shirt with bright shorts and black trainers. Jake looked like it was a cold, chilly day and he was dressed in jeans and a snowboarding jacket. Liam was complaining to Jake about Mrs Smith. Before I could tell them about the rock, Mira demanded that they tell us what they were talking about and what Mrs Smith was doing. *Really* Mira?

"Well, Jadie's dad asked me if I could pick up the envelope that he dropped," Liam began, "Then, you called me, and I accidentally put the volume on the walkie talkie to maximum sound! It was so loud! My hand slipped and I ended up pushing a bottle of chillies into a random dessert. Then, Mrs Smith came in and said that she wanted some peaches to try and test out a medicine that she invented, so Pau- I mean, Jadie's dad gave her the dessert. When she tried the dessert, she started wheezing and coughing! It was wonderful!" Liam explained, "Then, she got mad with me and told me that I was the culprit. Then, I ran here." He finally finished.

Then, I saw all three of them scrutinising the rock. I ran my finger over it but did not put any of my fingertips near the diamond shape inscribed on it. Mira noticed that I had not touched the diamond shape, so she asked, "Why won't you touch it? It doesn't bite."

"I'm not scared of it, but I don't think that touching a diamond shape or a strange shape that crashed into a dung heap is a good idea. Obviously, it had been kept there for a reason." I said, choosing my words carefully. I knew that a roar of laughter was imminent, but I didn't scowl when Mira rolled over, her face pink from giggles.

"It is a big pebble Jadie! Look! If you are not going to touch it, then I will!" She grinned, pressed the diamond and with that, it gave a tremble and rocks flew in different directions. I covered my face and shielded my eyes from the rocks. As we looked, we saw that a strange mist had covered a faint gleam where the diamond had been moments before. I gaped at it and exchanged discombobulated faces with Mira. Liam was first to speak, "Jadie, we must show your parents. This is something big and we must let the grown-ups know, this is so exciting!" It took all four of us to lift it just one inch off the floor. How was it so much heavier now? We went to my mum's office, and she was not in the mood for being disturbed, but as we showed it to her, the bright lights from the gem had gone. She marvelled at the pillar and spent an awfully long time scrutinising it from every possible angle. After many conversations and questions, she believed us and asked Miss Kettle, the cleaner to take it to the museum downstairs. She said that it was a truly awesome discovery, but we should all go to bed after dinner. I slipped the closest person a note which read:

Meet me after dinner. Museum. password: Levitation (mum's favourite word)

It turned out that the person was Liam and he mouthed

How did your mum not see you use the pen?

I shrugged and headed downstairs with the three of them. On the way, Mira gave me a look full of meaning which I didn't entirely understand. Then she slipped away. I left for dinner. On the way, I saw Mrs Smith, her sour, pale face contorted into a frown. She started to mutter about something. I did not stay long to listen. I gulped down a few sandwiches and a strawberry tart. I got my torch and ran towards the museum. A scanning machine said: password?

I grabbed a card from the pool and wrote with a marker nearby: levitation. I let it scan and the door swung open. The first thing I saw was Liam, pointing towards an eerie glow on the statue. We darted towards it. I was first to see the eerie writing on the side of the stone. I shone my torch on it while Liam read:

Is gem I to he curse of he an way

I didn't have the faintest idea what the writing meant as none of it made sense, but Liam was looking about for an archway. I had no idea how he had just known that way must mean archway. I was rather impressed. I was terrified with the thought of magic being real because for every bad thing, there is something good and every good thing has something bad. He suddenly jumped and grabbed my arm tightly. "Look Jadie! There's the archway!" he cried. I looked in the direction of his quivering finger. There, was a sinister looking archway which was carved with elaborate patterns. Liam started to step towards it and was ready to go under it, but I pulled him back.

"No! There is a curse Liam! Don't go near it!" I said, "Plus, we should figure it out with Mira and Jake as well, they're probably wondering where we are." Liam made a face. "Fine," he grumbled. We were on our way to the door, when we suddenly heard footsteps coming towards us. Closer and closer and closer. We froze and hid behind the ancient mummy sarcophagus and watched carefully as the footsteps got louder and louder. The footsteps were now right in front of us and yet we couldn't see who it was. I admit I was petrified. Liam seemed terribly excited. Ignoring my pale face, he looked around in the darkness and managed to get hold of an ancient blanket. We felt around and found three others. Just as thought we could hide under the blankets; Liam accidentally kicked me with his with his boots. Caught by shock, I got pushed down and hid behind a stuffed polar bear. Through the corner of my eye, I could see a dark, mysterious figure shining a torch. There were lots of objects pushed aside and a big lump lying underneath the blanket. As I was under the beast's tail, I was shocked that it was so heavy. I saw the figure advance towards the lump under the blankets. I watched in terror as the figure took out a knife and started to stab at the blanket. I shut my eyes tightly thinking that there was no way Liam could be alive. I had led him into a death trap. As the figure left, the tail seemed to slide off me. I heard it speak! That meant, it had to be…

"Liam!" I cried with relief as I saw he was spared. He gasped and groaned, rubbing his head, and looking reproachfully at the tail.
"Why did you have to hide under the tail? My head kept on banging against it! And your back is pure bone! Soo bony!" he complained. He walked over to the lump rather unsteadily. He pulled the blanket over his head and showed me lots of blankets underneath. They were ripped and torn to shreds.

How did you get away?" I asked.
"Well, I heard you moving and decided to follow. Why did you decide to go under its butt?" he said.
"I don't know! Anyway, since when did you weigh so much?" I asked.
"Oi!" he grumbled, "I am starting to wonder why I didn't pass the letter to Mira."
We started to head back. As we walked, we wondered who the figure was. Well one thing was for certain. This hotel was not safe. It had someone with a knife, someone who wanted to murder someone else. The someone didn't know that the someone else had escaped. Liam noticed nothing from my pale face which could have gone

transparent if it had got any paler. I said goodnight and slipped away. I had a troubled sleep, dreaming about an assortment of weird curses. I woke up sweating and found the blanket kicked off and the pillows at the foot of my bed. I got out of bed, got dressed and ready, and went out to get a glass of water.

"Liam!! What are you doing here so early?" I yelled, as I saw Liam chatting with my sister Lucy. He jumped. He had clearly not needed as much sleep and was ready to continue from yesterday's adventure. It was then that I saw Mira and Jake staring reproachfully at me through bloodshot eyes. I guess that he had already told them about last night and they didn't look happy as only he and I had gone, not they. I quickly got myself some breakfast and was ready to set out with my friends. And explain a few things to Mira and Jake of course.

As we went into the corridor, I felt happy to know that at least it wasn't just me who was half asleep. Mira was staring through half closed eyes while Jake was 20 metres behind us, literally sleep walking with his travel pillow. Liam sighed and elbowed him. "Look, I know that it is a teeny, weeny bit early in the morning and that you're grumpy that only Jadie and I had gone to the museum, but she," he threw me a furious look, "said that we should wait for you. Yeah, I am also SO sleepy, and I want to fall asleep on my pil-" he cried leaving his sentence incomplete and whirled around. "Justin!" he cried. Liam's brother, Justin was standing behind us. He looked very triumphant and sweaty.

"Just- fini-finished-th-the r-race!" he puffed.

Justin was not looking sleepy at all. However sleepy Jake was, he was a huge sports fan and his bleached hair, football T shirts and sports shoes showed it. He listened eagerly while Mira and I struggled to keep our eyes open. Liam was waiting expectantly.

"How did you do?" Jake asked the younger boy. Justin's eyes were filled with pride. "I was third!" he cried.

Jake clapped enthusiastically. Mira and I tried our best to clap along, but we were so sleepy that we could hardly lift our arms. I looked at Liam and saw that he was not clapping along but looking extremely unimpressed. I poked him.

"Why aren't you clapping for your own brother?" I scolded angrily.

"Because the other people he was against was Izzy L and Thomas B." he huffed.

"So, are they the slowest people in the hotel?" I asked, causing Jake's grin to fade as he looked at me incredulously, "Have you ever done racing with the running coach, AKA my dad?" he asked, "Your mum is the owner of this very hotel… Seriously, you don't know enough!"

"*What?*" I had no idea how the sports were run in the hotel.

"They pick people who are of the same running ability!" interrupted Liam angrily. I stared at him. "He came third out of three people!" Liam continued as if this was extremely obvious. A moment of stunned silence passed between Mira, Jake, and me. Then we burst out laughing.

"What? I still came third!" he pouted, "I am telling mummy!" he stormed off. Liam shook his head, "Typical."

3. Celebrations and deciphering

Once Justin went off to find his mum, we headed down to the museum. The sunlight was flooding in through the window. The museum was not exactly quiet. There was a buzz of talk outside the windows.

"Oh no." Mira murmured, but it was too late. A security man came and unlocked the doors after putting a glass cage over the archway and the rock.

"Oh… we were too late." Liam sighed, "Well, tomorrow I will wake you up an hour earlier, maybe two." The writing had strangely melted into the rock, and I received the same terrified feeling when I realised that magic was real last night.

The intricate patterns on the archway were now caked with mould. The doors opened and a flood of people entered the room. I saw that no one looked at anything else apart from the new stone that had just arrived. It did not help us at all to get near the stone. We had to wait until they would leave and go to something else. I looked around to talk to Liam but found that he had vanished. Mira and Jake had clearly noticed too as they were searching for him, calling his name.

After a bit, we found him, holding what looked like an orange lava rock. He ran past us, disregarding Mira's calls. I gave him a 'what- are -you -doing?' look but he ignored me and did something I would never have imagined him to do. He ran towards the statue and smashed the relic onto the floor! The security guard bent down to look at it while Liam plucked the key out of his pocket. Signalling for us to follow, he went towards the back of the archway cage.

"Liam! How could you?" I said angrily.

"What? Oh, that was a prawn cocktail that I got from lunch." He said, grinning slightly and running to the cage.

"Woah!" he gasped and pocketed the key. "Hey look! The rock is free! Come on!" he shouted as we raced to it. We were examining it closely when I smelt a horrid, whiffy smell that smelt like baccy from behind me. I jumped.

"Now honey, what are you doing eh?" came a voice from behind me, dripping with hatred.

"Mrs Smith!" I yelled.

"Honey, now, no need to be alarmed honey, I was just wondering if I could borrow you so that you could come and give a bit of breakfast to my pets?" she asked.

I gulped. Mrs Smith was famous for having a snake and knowing her, probably a cobra or some unidentified species that no one would want to know about.

She was wearing her grimy, grey apron and her hair was in an untidy bun. The greasy garment was stained with dirt. Breathing in the unpleasant fumes of her over-scented perfume, I hastily retreated, dragging Mira, Jake, and Liam with me.

"I am a bit busy now Mrs Smith." I smiled nervously.

I ran for my life. When she had said you can come and give a bit of breakfast to my pets, I thought she meant that I might be the breakfast for her pets.

When she calls me honey, I know that I'm in serious trouble not just like the detention types, but as in death.

"That stinking, idiotic, nosy, horrible, rude, twisted-" Liam began. I clamped my hand over my ears to spare myself from the torrent of filth that spewed from Liam's mouth.

"She's still here, we will have to try another time." Jake sighed cutting through Liam's insults. We all went to our rooms, but I was last and as I reached floor 6, the elevator doors clanked shut and it headed down 2 floors. The doors opened again to reveal Mira, white faced and petrified.

"Neither my mum nor dad is in the room! It is locked!" she wailed. I calmed her down and told her that we could both go to my mum's room and then, we would find hers. As I opened the door, I stared in surprise as my dad rushed out of the door, dressed in a blue tuxedo and his hair neatly combed. He asked me if I was off on another discovery investigation.

Before I could say anything, he laughed and ruffled my neatly combed hair and added a few matted knots. I grinned at him but the second he left, I scowled. I ran off into the room, Mira at my heels. We saw both mums chatting happily and applying coats of nail polish onto their glimmering nails. I saw Mira's mouth open in surprise for a second. My mum was wearing a dress made of a floaty, periwinkle-gold material. Mira's mum Mrs Pamela Partil was clad in a blue one, adorned with intricate patterns. My mum looked awesome, with shoulder-length black hair, a graceful neck, an amazing figure tucked into a beautiful dress. Mira's mum was also wearing black leggings along with her turquoise dress. She was wearing leather boots and had her silver charm necklace on.

"Why are you looking confused Jadie?" my mum asked, "You should know that today is the 200th anniversary of this hotel!" and she smiled.

Mira's mum stared at my mud-stained jersey; my tatty, battered shoes and my messy, tangled hair. She didn't say anything but pursed her lips. I felt a bit hurt. Mira got dressed into a rose-pink dress that swayed a lot, her hair was tied up into an elegant knot. While removing her trainers, Mira was talking rapidly, "You know the rock, well, I think that the type of the rock might be a rare one and the inside of it might be an extremely exotic gem! I have read all about it in "Miranda's guide to rocks and gems!" she cried excitedly.

"We will talk about it later!" Mrs Partil smiled. But for now, we must party!" she swept Mira out of the door and my mum did the same to me after taking an expensive camera out of a drawer. The four of us waited for the lift together. While we were waiting, I kicked myself silently for having forgotten about the hotel's grand anniversary party. My mum is the Head of the hotel and I had just behaved as if I didn't know how special this day was! As we stepped into the lift with our mums, Mira and I were talking furiously but softly.

"What do we do?"
"We have to see what both of them mean and stop Mrs Smith from whatever she is doing and also, find out what is wrong with her."
"What if she is magic too, like the archway and rock?"
"Then, we are doomed, and we hope for the best."
"Oh, that is nice."
"What is nice, girls?" asked my mum who seemed to be eavesdropping on us.

We gave an unconvincing grin and kept quiet until my mum asked again.

"The jar of cocoa powder that Jadie gave us last week." Mira hastily said.

"Oh, yes. That was wonderful! Thank you, Mrs Hills, that was delicious! Perhaps maybe…" then, they went back into deep conversation. As if a light bulb had lit inside my head, I had an excellent idea!

"Mira, as soon as the party starts and the group photos are taken, can you please go up to your room? I whispered.

"Why?" asked Mira.

"What are you whispering about girls?" asked my mum. I tried to hide a grimace. Ever since the rock crashed into my back yard, mum had always been suspicious of me.

"What types of food we would have in the party!" I said brightly.

"The dance moves for the party!" said Mira simultaneously. We glared at each other furiously.

"I mean, we mean what type of food we would have that would be alright to eat before we start dancing! We don't want to vomit!" I said with an unconvincing smile. They stared suspiciously at us before the doors clacked open and we hurried out.

"As you were saying, why should we go to my room?" Mira asked.

"I want to get some hot chocolate powder. I think that it will help us find the code". I cried. She gaped at me as if I had gone mad. I had tried my utmost to sound impressive and most of all, sane.

JADIE! YOU ARE MY BEST FRIEND BUT SOMETIMES, I THINK THAT YOU GO WELL… MAD! WE ARE SO CLOSE TO DISCOVERY AND YOU WANT A HOT CHOCOLATE! YOU DERANGED-" She began.

"Look, "I said, trying to sound reasonable. "I am not thirsty for hot chocolate, but I think that we can see the writing more clearly! After all, 'is gem I to he an curse of he way' does not make sense. Trust me Mira." I said.

"Still think that you are mad but… ok." She said at last. She dragged me by the arm to the party hall and unfortunately, we bumped into our parents. They were dancing along cheerfully and having the time of their lives. I noticed some people trip over their long dresses. All the peoples' dresses were making me feel queasy, the brightness of the garments was piercing my brain making it hard to see.

"Hey kids! You were planning some dance moves, weren't you? Well, we were hoping the DJ and dance team would arrive soon, but they seem to be delayed. You can lead the group. Go on." Mira's mum, Pamela said.

"I… er." I stammered, looking at Mira for help. She doesn't like dancing so I thought she would have some smart excuse up her sleeve.

"Sure! We would love to!" she grinned falsely and dragged me forward. Then, she tripped on her long dress and sprawled to the floor. No one else noticed except our mums.

"OH! Gosh! Mira dear!" her mother sobbed, acting over-dramatic as if Mira had died. Mira looked up slowly and started to cry, I was sure that it was fake as I saw no tear trickling down her cheek.

"I don't think that I can dance, but I do love dancing." Mira sobbed hysterically but convincingly. Now, I knew that she was definitely faking. I even saw a shadow of a smile unfold on the edges of her lips. I giggled. I couldn't help it.

"Jadie! Did you push her?" Pamela asked me rather coldly, noticing my grin. I fought to keep my face straight.

I shook my head earnestly.

"Well, please can you take her up to our family room and let her sit it out for a bit." She said angrily, shoving a bag into my stomach, knocking all the wind out of me. I stumbled to the ground.

"A bit more gently Pam.." my mother said.

"Sorry, it was by accident." Pamela muttered curtly. I knew that she just gets really stressed. I took Mira upstairs. Immediately she stopped crying and started to chuckle helplessly.

"I didn't think that they would actually fall for it!" she giggled.

We quickly went up to her room and immediately, she brought out the cocoa powder, not knowing why. We quickly grabbed the pot.

"Now what?" asked Mira. I only smiled and led her downstairs.

"No Jadie! We aren't allowed!" she screamed and tried in vain to go back but I dragged her through the barrier and into the museum.

"If we get caught..." she began warningly.

"Oh, don't worry," I said.

I told her to wait as I would quickly come back. Then, before she could do anything, I ran back to the party room and told my mum where we would be. I did not wait for her to answer, I just left. Then, I went back to Mira, who was standing in exactly the same spot and staring upwards.

"I don't like this. I *really* don't like this…"

I was not worried because my mum could call me when it was time for cake and drinks. That was in three hours.

Plenty of time I thought. I wanted to get my walkie talkie, but it was in my jersey pocket, far away. I wanted to call Jake and Liam through it. I then sneaked into the security guard's office, ignoring Mira's questions. I did this because I had an idea. I wondered if there were any walkie talkies inside. Luckily, there was. I knew that every walkie talkie in the hotel has a different number, so I quickly typed in Liam's.

"Yeah, what is it, wanting to see my new trainers? They are wicked!" Liam told me from the other end of the line, "Being friends with you and Mira has taught me that I should always expect anything, so I brought my walkie talkie in my tuxedo pocket." he said. I told him to come, and he came immediately. I guess that my mum was okay with us going to the museum, because she hadn't called us by now.

"Well, what did you find out?" Jake asked.
"We found out that Jadie adores cocoa powder." Mira grumbled.
"So, you called us to give you a hot chocolate?" asked Liam sarcastically.
"No! I will show you." I snapped, infuriated that they all thought that I was being strange. I took them to the statue and quickly unlocked the cage. Soon, we were running our hands over the heart of the statue, trying to get the emerald to present itself to us. We were unsuccessful. Liam kicked the sacred stone. I gasped, not in horror but in amazement, as the emerald came into view. Jake punched him on the back. Afterwards, all four of us pulled the stone out of the table and I sprinkled half of the jar on the writing.

No one else knew what I was doing. The silence hung on the air as I sprinkled. Looking up, I thought I saw a figure moving about in the shadows. I shook myself slightly. There were no ghosts here.

"Look! Can't you see the writing now?" I asked excitedly. They all nodded and gazed in amazement as I blew. The words that we could see were written in black ink but now, new letters appeared, forming a sentence.

"This gem will stop the ancient curse of the archway." I read out. The gem tingled and, in its reflection, I saw another face join ours and a figure knocking Mira, Jake and Liam out of the way.

"Thank you for figuring that out for me…" purred Mrs Smith, "So…hand the gem over, or *suffer* the consequences.

4. The curse

We quickly took shelter, desperate to escape from Mrs Smith. I cowered behind the stuffed rhino, whimpering quietly as Mrs Smith advanced towards me, her walking stick raised murderously in front of my startled eyes. She knocked the rhino out the way with surprising strength for someone who looked so frail. She let her plaited, grizzly hair swing. I felt panic clawing at my heart as the woman approached. I flung my hand over my face, ready for the blow that never came. I held it for about 20 seconds, but it felt like forever. When I dared to open my eye, if I still had one, I gave it a roll. I was alive. I looked at Mrs Smith, who was now tending to Mira, Jake, and Liam. That was strange, as I thought she looked more than capable of killing them a few minutes ago. Then, I saw my mum standing there by the door, staring straight into the room. Behind her, I saw some people from the medical bay. It must have all happened very quickly. I wondered who had called my mum and the medical staff. I ran to her as looked at me.

"Oh, you poor thing!" she cried. I stretched my arms wide, ready to hug her. To my indignation, she rushed past me and embraced the stuffed rhino.

"Oh, you poor thing. Adventurer Birch broke every bone in his body to get that! Well, almost…" she sobbed. Then, she turned to me.

"Are you ok?" she said, "I KEPT THAT BARRIER FOR A REASON JADIE!"

I looked at Mira for help, but she was knocked out cold.

"How did this happen Henrietta?" she asked.

"Oh, I don't know…" she lied, "I just came in when I heard screams. I think that they knocked into the horn of the rhino." she said. I glared. My mum didn't believe me when I said that I didn't want heavy food so that I would not puke and she believed a witch's tale of 3 children getting knocked out by a stuffed animal! The adults didn't let me talk. Mum gave me a choice: either I attend the party quietly or accompany the nurses as they took Mira, Jake, and Liam one at a time, to their rooms. I wasn't fooled. I could see that she clearly wanted 'the kids out of the way.' I didn't care. I wanted to see them get taken to their rooms. I was extremely annoyed with Mrs Smith as it was now more than once that she had stopped our investigations. I clutched the emerald tightly in my fist. When my mum wasn't looking, I quickly put the gem into the empty diamond shape in the statue. It immediately closed. Then, I followed the nurses up the elevator. I watched as the nurses took the other stretcher out to Jake's room. They all went to Jake's room as his mum had offered to care for them until they woke up. My mind was racing. What was wrong with that lady? She couldn't be human; she took this whole magic affair so easily! She even seemed to walk in the shadows! No wonder I could not see her, and she was spying on us. I felt rather lonely as there was no one to talk to. All three of my friends were lying knocked out, in Jake's room. My mum decided I better go to bed. It was strange seeing my friends knocked out, but I was sure, they would be fine the next day and we could pick up from where we left.

The next day, I woke up after having a satisfying dream about a stuffed guinea pig eating Mrs Smith and me controlling it. I woke up and went to the bathroom. I changed into a scruffy, rather tight turquoise jumper with black leggings. I had no pockets in that jumper, so I decided to take my red bag stuffed with my special items
-Torch
-Whistle
-Knife

-Rope
-Compass
-Walkie talkie pair

And Mira's suggestion
-Camera
And something that Jake would probably want:
-A case full of sandwiches, bottles, and cookies.

I hoped the kitchen staff wouldn't notice all the things that had gone missing. I also hoped that this solved Jake's problem of always being hungry. I set off towards Mira's room, before remembering last night's incident, and hurried off to Jake's instead. His family were in number 124, so I had to use the lift. I spent many seconds of uncomfortable silence in the lift as Mrs Smith was in the lift as well. Why didn't you take the stairs? I thought to myself desperately. As soon as the door clanked open, I dashed out, almost immediately bumping into someone and fell over.

"Ouch look out." cried Mira. I was so glad to see that she was up and about.

"Sorry." I said from the floor, "Are you okay now, Mira? How are the boys?"

Mira explained that they all felt much better, and Jake's mum had really looked after them well. Jake's mum had set out now, confident that the three of them were fit to face the day.

"Mrs Smith was so nasty!", I continued.

"What? No. Your mum said that the rhino knocked me out when I bumped into it. Mrs Smith tried to help us, which does not seem entirely right..." she began, frowning slightly.

"Of course, it's not true. She knocked you out with her cane. My mum only came after you got knocked out. That is what Mrs Smith told her, but I saw everything. She knocked you out with her walking stick and tried to take the emerald!" I told her angrily.

Mira's memory seemed to come back.

"Oh! Yes! Now I remember!" she cried, "Let's go and tell the others." We headed back, and Mira told me that she had gone looking for me as soon as Jake's mum told her what had happened. We soon got to room 124 and saw Liam on one bed and Jake on the other. We decided to go to Liam first.

"We will go nice and quietly." I said to Mira.

"No thanks. WAKE UP, LIAM WEST!" she yelled. He jerked awake immediately. His eyes were not entirely open. He checked his watch grumpily.

"It's 2a.m.!" he complained. I was not exactly liking Mira's approach of waking people up.

"No! It is 2p.m.!" she cried, checking her own watch, which read 14:00. Liam groaned. "Can you wake up Jake first next time?" he grumbled. We hurried to wake Jake as Liam fell asleep again. Mira plays the clarinet and for some odd reason, her mum had left it in its case at the foot of Jake's bed. She sighed and grabbed it, pieced it together and blew loudly in his ear. It was so loud that the people above, below, to the left and to the right of the room, screamed along with Jake and Liam. Mira put it away as I glared at her.

Thirty minutes later, we were running back to the museum. "This time that nosy, old woman won't disturb us," cried Mira. I knew that you had to pull the museum doors from the inside, so from the outside, you must push. So, we blocked them from the inside and made sure that no one could get in. I made Mira and Liam (after a lot of groans and moans) push a massive sarcophagus against the door. We all wanted to study the stone in peace.

"So, the archway would curse us if we went under it." said Liam, looking fascinated. We were about to take a photo of both things in case Mrs Smith came and disturbed everything when Mira went to check on the door. She pushed the sarcophagus against the door and turned back to us.

"What's so bad about Mrs Smith?" asked Jake, who hadn't been told what really happened yesterday.

"Oh, Mrs Smith came and tried to murder us and take the emerald" I muttered, distracted by a particular pattern on the archway, which looked like Latin. We took a photo with my camera and got ready to copy the intricate designs on the archway into Liam's sketch book. I was feeling very happy and was surprised that Jake hadn't said…

"I am very hungry!"

Great. I brought out the bag full of snacks that were one family pack of cookies, sandwiches and two bottles of water. After he had finished the whole family pack, Jake wanted another. Then, I had an idea.

"Sure, take a slice of cake" I said. He scooped it out of my bag and put the whole thing into his mouth. Then, his grin sagged and was replaced with an expression of utter horror. He started to cough and wheeze before drinking the whole bottle of water.

"SPICY!" he screamed.

"Chilies." I smiled. After that, Jake had rather lost his appetite for snacks.

We were just identifying the rock when the door banged open. Mira, Jake, and Liam glared at me. The door opened inwards. I had made them push the heavy sarcophagus against the door for nothing. Mrs Smith climbed over the sarcophagus easily and strutted towards us, whistling. As Mira, Jake and I backed against the wall, Liam took out the food bag. He threw our other bottle of water on her and while she was pushing her hair out of her eyes, he sprinkled some of the leftover crumbs on her. He told us to run. We ran as fast as we could towards the door but somehow, she reached before us. We backed against the wall. Jake grabbed Mira and tried to get Liam, but he had slipped on the water on the floor. Panicking, Mira pulled Jake towards the exit, and they looked back at us. Well, me. Liam had picked himself up, and he and Jake started to run. They tried to get Mira, but she was intent on getting me. She ran back to me just as Mrs Smith rose, her normally watery blue eyes were now red and gleaming like fire, and a mad grin on her face. I stepped back in alarm, colliding into a colossal bull which was standing behind me. Mrs Smith whipped a bottle out of her red handbag.

"Yessss. Child! A smart one like you should have probably known by now that there is magic in the air. It has found me, and it will destroy you," she hissed, coming closer and closer. I did not know what to do. The potion was seconds away from falling on me. It was literally one centimetre away from my face. I cowered pitifully, covering my face with my hand. I thought that this was the end.

"Aaaahhhh!" yelled Mira. Brave, stupid Mira, trying to help me. She should have run with the others. Normally, she is wise. The witch (I decided to call her that after everything she told me) didn't spare us. She whipped the bottle out of her hand and poured it on the floor. The second Mira stepped on it, she flew, landing right underneath the cursed archway.

5. Secrets

I yelled in shock and horror as a blinding flash of light surrounded Mira. Her eyes were not open, and her body was limp. The light had blasted me and Mrs Smith off our feet. Mrs Smith uncorked the bottle and let the swirling, green liquid tether over the brink.

"Right, start talking. How do you get the emerald?" she snarled. I kept my mouth shut, rather pleased that I could do something that a witch couldn't. The proud feeling melted away when I saw the label on the bottle:

-Losing mind
Some of the others read:
-Body flipped inside out
-Instant death
-Werewolf
-Turn into a verruca

And many more. Those were some of the nicest ones.

"OOH! Feisty, are we? I have tried to be nice" she whispered.

"Nice? How? You almost killed me! The curse on her could be death!"

I yelled, pointing to Mira's lifeless, dead-looking body.

"Maybe! Well, I have been nice by not killing you the moment you were born, I hope that you appreciate that. And for the times when I see you out and about in the hotel." she spoke. She then let one drop of liquid drip, not onto me but on the bull that I was standing in front of. It gave a little tremble and slowly, its glassy eyes blinked. I ran for my life. The creature chased me until I climbed over the sarcophagus and scrambled over. But the witch was too fast. She put one drop of the same liquid on the sarcophagus. I stood, paralysed in horror as the mutilated face yawned and started to grab at me with scabby fingers. I watched in terror as the mummy started to unwrap its bandages. I didn't know what I would see if I stayed any longer. I did not. I ran and I ran until I reached the lift. Then I stopped. I hadn't waited for Mira. She had just risked her life for me but I hadn't done the same. I was a coward. A huge wave of guilt crashed into me, and I felt terrible for leaving her. I couldn't believe I had escaped the terror. My heart was beating fiercely in my chest. I hoped that Mira would escape too. We would have a lot to talk about at dinner. I pressed the lift button repeatedly and angrily. It was taking ages!

Unfortunately, Mr Jacks saw me. "Miss Hills, it is hard enough to tolerate your presence, but seeing your abnormally red face gives me true horror. You look like a thoroughly embarrassed tomato." he snapped, looking disgusted as he saw my red face. "Go and help your father with the dinner tonight".

I ran away just as the lift doors opened and went to find my dad. He was sticking labels on to the plates.

"Oh yes, that Mrs Smith will be furious if I make the food ONE minute late. I'd better get it ready now and set an alarm. Mr Brown wanted to have pineapples on his pizza instead of pepperoni, I shouldn't forget that. And then I better take Mr River's lasagne out of oven before it burns, and Mr Jim's rice needs to be very spicy..." he was muttering. Then, he saw me and smiled.

"Jadie! If you don't mind dear, could you see when the guests come and alert Diana - you know, the waitress" he said. I did as I was told and at every minute, some guests would arrive, and I would have to alert Diana. She was rather annoyed, as I kept coming back to her every twenty seconds. Jake and his family came soon, and he asked me what happened after he left. He also apologised for running away and looked shame-facedly at the carpet. I told him that Mira had got kicked under the archway (He gasped and turned pale) and that it was Mrs Smith who had magical powers (he nodded as if he had expected this the whole time). He came to me and told me that Liam's parents along with his would be sitting together and Liam, Jake, Justin (Liam's brother), and Jake's brother would be sitting together. So, Jake could pass on the horrifying news. Liam came soon after and asked me the same question. I told him that Jake would tell him. Mrs Smith was the last to arrive and her evil grin caused my stomach to drop. I quietly put her food on the table. I knew that I would be in peril if I stayed too long so I turned to run. But she was too fast, even with her appearance of a middle-aged lady, she was quick to stop me. As I looked into her eyes, they gleamed red again. She seized me by the collar.

"If you utter one word to anyone about me, and this counts for your Liam and Jake people, magic will mix this into your bones." She purred, bringing a bottle that read "Instant Death" out of her handbag. "Now, run along dear. If you would prefer it, I will send them a note. In fact, I will." She said sweetly. By the time everyone had sat down, my parents had come. My sister was there as well.

"Well, run along!" she grinned. My heart was thumping painfully. We had a private table with a butler and waitress to ourselves. It had comfortable cushions and elaborately painted seats. I sat on mine and began to wolf down my noodles. My sister was already there, playing a game on her phone. Then, my dad stood up. He looked around.

"Where is your friend Mira and her family?" he said.

I swear that I saw Mrs Smith's face, a smoky figure, behind my dad. Her eyes were filled with warning. "Oh, they went out today." I invented. I hadn't the faintest idea where she could be. Then through the closed door, I saw the two boys waving a piece of paper to me. I finished rapidly and dashed out to meet them.

"What is this?" Jake said. I saw this on the table." He read it with difficulty.

You are not to tell anyone about the little bit of drama. If you dare not keep this a secret amongst yourselves, you will suffer a painful death. Try it and I shall simply modify the memory.

"Let's go back to the museum soon. Bring a torch and a camera." said Liam.

I nodded at them. I quickly finished dinner, got a cheesecake, and rushed off because Mrs Smith was now walking towards our table. She and my dad are friends, so my parents were happy to have a chat. I quickly ran off, Jake and Liam right behind me. We took the elevator to the museum. Everything looked the same. The Mummy and the Bull were in their right places. A limp figure was underneath the archway.

"Mira!" I cried and hurried over to her. But I found the Mummy, its rotten, bloodstained bandages reeking terribly, out of its sarcophagus, laid where Mira had a been a few hours ago. I started to feel guilty as I had naively assumed that Mira had escaped as I did.

"We have to search for her.", I cried, and we searched everywhere in the museum. The first place was the sarcophagus because Liam thought that the Mummy and Mira could have been swapped. We checked there and it was empty. We were starting to worry when Jake had an idea.

"Maybe Mrs Smith took Mira to her room?" said Jake. I thought that it was indeed possible, and Liam agreed too. We went to the number 609 which was opposite the annexe that we stayed in. Then, we stopped.

"We need a key.", said Liam. We rushed back down and sneaked into the receptionist's office. She was out at 'Dine with Mine'. So, we quickly got the key. Using the stairs, we reached Mrs Smith's room. We put the key into the lock, turned it… But the door did not open. It stayed shut!

"Well, did you think that I would really let you walk in like that?", snarled a gleeful voice from behind me. I was nose to nose with Mrs Smith.

"Have you already forgotten that I have eyes everywhere, child?", she growled. "Young Miss Partail was always in danger; she was too loyal to you. Why, it was me who thought she was under the blanket, and now, no one will ever know! Ah yes, stand still and don't try to tell anyone what I am doing. Magic will bind you to the secret that I will tell you." Immediately, all of us felt a tingling sensation as if we had just promised something in a very magical way.

"I guess that now, I am free to tell you all my secrets. It would be necessary to tell you, so that you are aware of how powerful I truly am. Not that ridiculous old lady in the dirty apron. You have promised not to tell anyone!" she chuckled gleefully. She looked at us once more and seemed convinced. "Now that the matter is settled, I will tell you my true name. Nephia Everdark. I have a gift in potion making, I have made nearly every one that is real! Except, of course, the nice ones. And they are all here!" She showed us the contents of her bag, where the gleaming bottles lay. "Mrs Henrietta Smith sounds far too… silly for a trained sorceress like me. Even Nephia Everdark seems way too happy and sweet but that is the name magic bestowed upon me and I must be grateful for it." She purred, "Now…" she took out a winking, red bottle out of her bag and splashed the contents around us. The liquid refilled itself almost immediately. Then, she started to melt. It was horrifying, her body oozing away into nothing but a queer, pale puddle on the floor. Then, it began to rise, taking another form, stranger and more terrible than before. It had thin, angular cheekbones with gleaming, crimson eyes. She had dark hair, cascading down like a waterfall. There was a grey, eerie looking mark on her palm which looked like a spear. She was clad in a flowing, dark cloak.

"This is my true form dears. I come from a different world. A different planet. I am what you kids call an alien. Oh, and by the way, I need the emerald. It will help me make the final potion which will give me the power to control the earth! This is the ultimate power." We tried to get out of the circle of liquid that had spewed onto the floor but there was literally an invisible door blocking us. Then, Nephia vanished, and I heard a door slam before we were left alone in the corridor. We turned to go before the circle vanished and a silhouette that looked like Mira slowly appeared on the floor. The silhouette began to gain flesh and started to stir.

"Got to warn… Nephia Everdark…what is going on," murmured Mira.

We bent down to Mira and gently tried to wake her. We realised that we couldn't see Nephia anymore, so we just focussed on waking Mira and getting out with her.

"Jadie!! Jake!! Liam!!" Mira cried, jumping up, "Wow, what is that?" continued Mira.

"… Your shoes", Liam replied uncertainly.

"Wow… what is that?", Mira asked again.

"Ummm… that's the wall…" I said.

It seemed that she had forgotten most of the things in the hotel. So, we quickly showed her everything in the hotel. We started reminding Mira of everything… the corridors, the hotel, the food. Slowly, Mira's memory came back. She even started to abuse Mrs Smith a bit. Then, as the topic moved on to the museum, Jake thought of something.

"Mira, what was the last thing that you remember?", he asked. I knew what he was thinking. Mira could have heard Nephia's plans. She shook her head. Then, her face brightened, and she said "Oh yes! I remember! Mrs Smith put me into this weird archway and there was lots of light. Then she drank some weird liquid and turned into nothing." We glanced at each other.

"Did she mention her name? Nephia Everdark?" Jake questioned. I was very relieved that Mira was alright, but I was anxious to know what the curse was as it was certainly not memory loss. Jake and Liam asked Mira lots of questions, but I stood quietly as my mind was whirling.

We warned her to act normal with her family as it was now getting late, and we were all meant to get back to our own rooms. We agreed to meet back early in the morning.

Next morning, I was obviously running late. Suddenly, I saw Mira and Jake. They were half-running, half-waddling in their wetsuits along the corridor, "It starts in five minutes! Meet me by the beach!" I knew that it was their surfing club and I carried on walking.

I don't go to surfing club. I prefer to walk in the courtyard and stare into the pond. I thought I may as well go back to my room for a rest. I ran to my bed and buried my head into the soft pillows. I was starting to feel calmer when someone very heavy started to sit on my ankles. "Ahhhh" Lucy!!" I yelled, my ankles throbbing.

"Sorry!!" murmured Lucy, sitting on the coffee table now. Lucy was prepared for a chat, but I just wanted to dwell in my own thoughts. So, I stealthily escaped into the courtyard. In a few minutes, I was sitting on a bench watching nothing in particular. Then I jumped off the bench and onto another one, much to the disapproval of 2 teenaged girls who were disturbed from their gaming on the phones. As they swapped disgusted looks, I carefully raised my foot and placed it on the wall behind them. I then hoisted myself up and managed to balance on the narrow wall… for two seconds. "Arrghhh!" I screamed as I lost my balance and fell onto the footpath below. I would have broken every bone in my body if it were not for two things:
1. The wall wasn't that high
2. I fell on someone who was passing below.

"Jadie! You are the most careless, dangerous, risk taking, annoying person!" Mira yelled. It turned out that I had fallen on her. I exclaimed "Oops", but Mira was clearly looking for something more than "Oops". She swung off her bag which contained fossils, rocks and heavy books and started to whack me with every word she said. "What-do-you-think-you-are-doing?" she yelled. Then, Jake came to my rescue. "Mira! That's enough... just shut up!" he yelled. He had appeared from nowhere and had grabbed Mira's bag. I stared, bewildered as Jake restrained Mira from slapping me anymore. He was still talking.

"Oh, today we were going to be surfing with dolphins, and then picking some special rocks from the seabed. Mira couldn't because when we measured her, she was 2 cm below the minimum height. It was so puzzling as I'm sure she was 3 cm above the minimum height last week", explained Jake. I understood why Mira was in such a bad temper, and sympathised. Those were two of Mira's favourite activities and she couldn't do them. And then, my heart was filled with dread as I realised that it was not simply just that. Mira had received the shrinking curse. I gasped with utmost horror. I told Jake and Mira what I thought. Mira looked at her hands and feet in terror, while Jake's eyes widened. He drew out his camera. "A few days ago, I noticed that there was some ancient Latin on the archway. I managed to translate it with an ancient languages app. It said that the shrinking curse will shrink its victim until he shall be smaller than a dust particle. It acts within a week!"

Mira went white with fear. I thought that she would have become transparent if she got any paler. "Do you mean... In a week, I will really be smaller than dust?" asked Mira in a quiet, fearful voice. We stayed silent for a moment.

"Nope, you 100 PER CENT WILL NOT!" Jake told her," Because we will get the emerald before the end of next week." She nodded hopefully.

I felt surreal as I remembered how Mira had saved me and she ended up getting cursed herself. "Hey, Mira. Thank you so much for saving my life. I am sorry that it had to happen to you." I told her gratefully. She didn't answer and looked expressionless.

Then, she pressed a little, blue stone into my hand. "I collected this while walking back from the club, I found it lying in a small box on the shore. Your mother will want it onto the display." she told me. "Don't lose it. It is really precious to me." And she rushed off, probably to throw up in anxiety.

I had a look at it and saw that the stone was a hue of blue. I didn't want to let Mira down and ever lose it, so I slipped it into my pocket. Jake gaped at it in awe and nudged me proudly. I was not expecting the nudge and the gem slipped out of my hand. I fumbled and tried to catch it but missed. I watched as if it was in slow motion as the precious stone tumbled down towards and then into the drain. I gasped as I heard the splash of the little pebble, into what I imagine would be murky and dirty sewage water. I screamed in horror. Jake and I both looked in despair and screamed "Noooooo!". I knew that the drains led to one massive hole in the ground, and if I could get there, I had a chance of saving the precious gem. I felt that I had let Mira down. There were many reasons to chase that stone. We couldn't just lose it. I felt awful.

6. Nephia's room

My scream of horror never left me. I had felt some sort of connection to this object as though it would be significant to our friendship. Mira had entrusted me with it. I knew that I could go to the drain hole near Courage Square. We hurtled past shops, knocking over onion crates and tomatoes on the floor. We ran through washing lines and came out wearing odd clothes. I laughed when Jake came out wearing a 2-year old's dress embroidered with sequins. He got his turn to laugh when I came out dressed in a pig's costume. Soon, we arrived at Courage Square, and I saw a little ladder descend into the gloomy crevice on the floor. It was a crooked, grimy one. I shone my torch into the gloom and spotted Mira's pebble down below. It had fortunately got caught on one of the protruding rocks at the bottom. It now stood innocently, gleaming with the light of my torch.

"Come on", I said to Jake. But he was retreating slowly.
"Jake! Are you claustrophobic or scared of the dark?" I snapped. He shook his head, turning a fearful shade of puce.

"Are you scared of a pebble?" I continued, raising my eyebrows, and rolling my eyes.
"It is not that! Let me ask you a question……" he began.
"No! You tell me why you don't want to go!" I interrupted.
"Fine! There are rats down there! Anyway, why are you risking your life in the sewers for a pebble?" he questioned rather meaningfully.

"I am not going down for a pebble! I am going down for Mira and guess what, I don't like it either, but she is my friend and I know it means something to us. We may even be able to swap it with the emerald." I said angrily. Jake looked like he had an answer but did not want to say it aloud. If I had hesitated, I probably wouldn't have gone down. But I didn't give myself a choice.

Without pausing, I quickly climbed down. My hands slipped quite a few times and several moments were spent clinging to the ladder with my eyes shut tight. After some time, I found the bottom of the hole and picked up the pebble. It stood out among the gloom, glowing in the light of my torch. Then, quite suddenly, my tool of light flickered out and died. I gulped. But that didn't matter too much. I could climb up without the torch. As my hand reached towards the ladder my fingers closed on thin air. A cold fist closed around my heart as I stumbled forward into the darkness. The glaring daylight above had vanished. I put my hand in my pocket to check if there was a matchbox or another torch. All I found was a what felt like a notebook and a jar. I had forgotten to put my emergency items into my pocket. I felt careworn and tired; the darkness seemed to be impenetrable and endless. When I looked up, I saw nothing above. I panicked and could hardly keep my eyes open. The darkness seemed to be engulfing me, I found it hard to draw breath. My legs felt like lead. It was so strange, I struggled for a few more seconds to try and find the ladder. I failed, and my legs suddenly buckled and collapsed with the gem in my hand.

"Owww, stop poking me." I mumbled. I was vaguely aware that I was alive. Slowly, I opened my right eye and looked around, I was still near Courage Square. I saw a freckled face, two brown eyes, a waterfall of matted hair before I heard my name. I sat up and saw Mira. She seemed to have shrunk. Looking closer, I realised she only went up to my chest. Jake was there too, feeding me something terribly bitter. To my great surprise, I saw Liam having an argument with his little brother Justin, about his fringe.

"Honestly Justin! If you don't have a haircut, you are going to look like – JADIE!" I heard Liam saying to him.

"If I don't cut my hair, I am going to start looking like Jadie?" Justin asked, confused," Geez! I will ask mum! I do not want to look like Jadie." He yelled, before seeing that I was awake and grinning sheepishly. I sat up, bolt upright. Jake pointed to some boys I hadn't seen before.

"These boys were walking by, and I called them to help. They managed to get you up." Jake told me. I was not in the mood for asking him why he couldn't have done it himself. I was surprised that the rescue had been so simple.

"How?' I asked.

"Dunno." Liam shrugged," Ask them." I got up and looked at Mira, she was alarmingly small. Just about 3 feet. She was straining her neck to look at me, her eyes filled with fear yet amazement. I walked over to the two boys who were now playing with a nerf gun.

"Um…hi. What's your names? And er… thanks for helping me. What exactly happened?" I asked approaching them quietly.

"Oh. Hi. Good to see you up and about. I'm Ethan and this ugly fella here is Griffin." He paused and put down his nerf gun to talk to me, "Well… we were walking by and then-OUCH! Hey! I'm talking to someone here!" he cried turning round angrily to face his friend. The boy called Griffin had shot him right in his ear.

"Well hurry up slowpoke! Otherwise, I'll shoot you in your eyeball!" snapped Griffin.

"You're asking for it…" growled Ethan before snatching up his gun and firing all his bullets at Griffin. We decided to leave this conversation and go back to our hotel and politely invited our new friends to come and see us sometime. I hadn't really had a chance to chat with them. I was still in a daze.

We went back to the hotel. I was tired and wanted to get changed. I lumbered up to my room and changed into a neat, blue dress with a comfortable collar. I hurried back to meet my friends.

Just as I was heading out into the corridor, Jake stopped me and said that he wanted to tell me something.

"Ethan and Griffin saw Nephia.", he blurted out.
"What??" I exclaimed in shock and bewilderment.
"Griffin said that he thought he saw an old lady running away into the shadows and she sort of melted away into the darkness. Then, there was a flash and Ethan saw a creepy figure standing a few metres away, then, when he looked again, there was nothing. They thought they had gone mad but found it strange that both had seen funny things. I joked and tried to make them ignore it." he explained.

I nodded and we started walking silently, deep in thought. Mira was waiting for me, and she was white with fear. Her body looked rather disturbing as her face showed the bright one of an eleven-year-old, but her body had shrunk. We had to get to the museum and get the gem before something happened. We brainstormed for ideas.

We wanted to cover up for now but were indeed worried how to confront Mira's mum. In the end, Liam thought that we should put her in his cousin's pram for now and think hard on what to do next. Mira protested so we did a vote. Liam immediately said that he wanted Mira to go in the pram, and made Jake reluctantly agree. I could not bear to look at Mira's tortured face, but I knew that it was up to me. And I knew she had to be safe. I unwillingly said 'yes'. Mira's hopeful face slumped down into a moody scowl. Liam gave me a "high five" and rushed off. With an apology to Mira, Jake ran off as well.

I gave Mira a sheepish smile. I wanted to update Mira on what Jake had just told me. "Oh Mira, by the way, Jake told me something. Apparently, Griffin and Ethan saw a shadow in the darkness that disappeared in an instant." I blurted out, still thinking hard.

"Well, that is very helpful" she said sarcastically.

"Ok, well I guess that is not very helpful so…" I told her everything and now, she seemed interested, the colour slowly coming back into her face. Then, Jake and Liam came back, and her face turned whiter with either fear or rage.

"I am *not* going in *that.*" She growled, glaring at the pram. It looked rather mouldy and battered, with faded, pink flowers.

"All right, chill!" Liam shouted," There was one more and it was blue and had dragons on it." Liam grinned and said he had seen it in the 'Lost and Found'.

"I want that one NOW!" Mira shouted. I have never seen Mira in a tantrum, and I didn't like it very much. I ran off to get her pram. Blue was Mira's favourite colour and dragons were one of Mira's favourite animals. I went back to the room and heard Mira complaining about how mouldy the pink pram was. She was saying that it was stinky and worse than a pigsty. She was even complaining that the blankets were ragged and that someone had vomited inside. She was trying in vain to stop Jake and Liam dragging her towards it.

"Ta Da!" I cried triumphantly and brought the blue pram from 'Lost and Found'. Mira gave a cry of delight and was able to take comfort in that it was her favourite shade of blue and had a ferocious dragon at the top. She struggled to climb in as she was still a bit big for the pram.

"Ah! It is perfect! The blankets are nice and cosy, the pillows are so warm and perfect!" she smirked snugly. She looked too pitiful to be made fun of. After all, she could be turned into a dust particle in six days. I decided to wheel Mira around first. I was so slow that I got lost from the boys.

I knew that we were all planning on heading to the museum, so I swiftly pushed her to the lifts. Mira was chattering away until we saw that the lift was occupied by her parents.

"Have you seen my Mirakins?" Her mother asked me.

"Uh… last time I saw her, she was at her club." I spoke.

"Which one?" she asked.

"Er- Basket-bye!" I said and rushed off to the café as soon as the lift opened.

"What type of club is Basket bye? I am pretty sure it was basketball." she said as I was trying to run away.

"Since when did you get another sister?" she yelled after me. "She isn't my sister!" I shouted out as I tried to escape.

I eventually found the boys and handed the pram to Liam as he rolled her towards the museum. I was starting to wish that there was no such thing as the museum because otherwise, none of this would have happened.

"Gosh, Mira! Did you know that your appearance has reduced by size, but your weight certainly hasn't!" Liam groaned.

"It has nothing to do with my weight! You have put that button-thingumabob on, so it is in parking mode, you need to push it up!" she snapped, her eyes filled with thunderous indignation.

As we reached the museum, with Liam and Mira still bickering, we realised with sinking hearts that it had been closed. There were safety ropes all over the entrance and a huge flashing red sign read:

CLOSED BECAUSE OF DESTRUCTION. MORE INFO FROM SECURITY. ROOM 2.

"Oh, that it splendid! All that for THIS! This horrid museum is closed!" he moaned. Then, he caught my eye, "OH, sorry, didn't mean that, apologies." He grinned sheepishly.

"It's fine, if it wasn't for this place, none of this would ever have happened." I sighed.

"Ye' ok luv?" a beefy man came from behind the counter. He was wearing an orange, glowing uniform and was covered in dirt while his mates were working furiously behind him.

"Ye wun o' those people who wan' info?" he said, lumbering over to me, "Ay, long story eh? Well, little boy came along, managed to open u' the sarcophagus! Would you believe it gal? Managed to throw it on the floor and, Oh Dang! He even pushed the big statue from the Mexican area! Unbelievable, incredible, I er... I er... No offence Miss!" he told me, "And smashing boots!" he grinned. I spared one look at my new footwear, "How could it happen?" I burst out. He sighed, "One momen' miss," and disappeared into a nearby door.

Mira sighed and whispered to me. "A lot has been going on recently. Now that we know her secret, Miss. Irritating Smith can make us become curious and investigate. It could be a trap!" she said. I agreed.

"Hey, darlin'," the man said, coming back again, "I can give you and your friends a tour, if ye please. Another woman is coming, name's Mrs Smith, perhaps you…" he started. We didn't want to listen to another word. We excused ourselves and ran off before she came and almost ran into her. I let go of the pram accidentally and Jake luckily caught it. He yelled 'go' and I went alone. I bumped into Mr Jacks, who was carrying a ceramic plate of crumpets.

"What on- Hills, clean those crumpets off the floor and make some new ones! 2 with Nutella on, 3 with butter and 1 plain. NOW!" he shouted angrily.

"I am in a serious rush, Mr Jack in a bo- I mean, Mr Jacks!" I cried.

"Why?" he asked.

"Got to call my uncle!" I cried.

"Your uncle is in the hotel; would you like me to take you?" he asked smoothly.

"No- my other uncle- dad's brother!" I invented wildly. He seemed on the point of agreeing when he shook himself slightly.

Right Miss Hills, I know your father well and I know he has NO siblings. You have lied to me. Come to my office immediately." He purred in a satisfied manner.

"Ok! I was lying. I feel ashamed of myself. I am a liar! I must make your crumpets." I said, crossing my fingers. I asked again and again. He finally agreed and left me to it. I had forgotten about my friends and reached my dad's cooking room. He smiled pleasantly but said that I could not use his room at this time. I dashed to my dad's colleague, Mr. Quinten's area office. He was the baker. He happily allowed me to make the crumpets.

"Yes, Missus, Mr Jacks had asked me to make them once before, here is the recipe."

He passed me a scroll of paper. I read it and thought *Nah… I'm not going to bother; I'll just get some from the cupboard.* I reached out my hand into the cupboard and brought out a new bag of crumpets. I popped them inside the toaster, and it seemed like forever when they finally came out. I grabbed them and put butter and Nutella on some. Feeling proud with myself, I shoved the plate into Mr Jack's hands and darted off. As I left the kitchen area and entered the dining area, I tripped over something and fell.

"Miss Hills, do you think that our guests like you lying in the middle of the breakfast room?" A familiar voice came from nearby. I saw Henry Jones, the saucepan scrubber standing near me. I swiftly got up and dashed off, leaving Henry to wipe the floor as well as the saucepans.

"Come back here, you lunatic!" he yelled.

I found Jake waiting for me nearby. I told him what had happened after I came out of the museum. *He* said that I was a lunatic!

Soon, we found Liam and Mira.

"Any plans?" asked Mira. She was already quite small. I hoped that it would slow down towards the end. I shook my head. Just then, Liam's brother, Justin came and told him that he needed to come for dinner. Liam moodily went downstairs. I looked out of the window. The moonlight flooded in, casting shadows around the walls. Was it my imagination, or was one, possibly in the shape of a human, slightly darker than the rest... and was it... moving? I shook my head and thought that I was hallucinating.

"We could get into trouble! I have heard that they want the troublemakers to help clean the museum! That is the new type of punishment." Mira cried eagerly. Jake and I looked uneasily at each other.

"Look, Mira, we both really would…love to ask if we can help at the museum clean… but you can't do anything while …you're… you're looking like this. I don't think that it is a good idea." Jake stammered.

"Oh, ok." She stared at the floor miserably.

"Oh, I think that it is a wonderful idea!" came a delighted shriek from the shadows.

"Right, I actually like staying with my parents." Jake murmured to Mira. She didn't answer. Nephia appeared from the shadows.

"It is called shadow walking. My great grandfather taught it to me. Marvellous skill, hard to master." She brushed off the dirt from her shoulder.

"Haven't seen you in a long time. Where is your friend? Is he gone or can I get rid of him?"

Mira and Jake were glaring at her, so I hastened to follow.

"I may not have told you enough, but I am looking for that emerald. It is of valuable importance. If I can get it, then it will mean that I will have power over the whole Earth. I need it, I need it!" she was now screaming. "Yes, I know it cannot bring back the dead or cannot disintegrate people with a single stare but at least I will be more powerful than the Earth!" she said, grimacing at the fact that she could not destroy the Earth yet.

"Oh, and Miss Hills," she called softening her tone. I reluctantly turned to her, "I put a potion on little Miss Mira after you fled from the museum. Basically, only the people who Mira wants to see the effect of the curse will see it that way. It's just to avoid questions. It's in Mira's control and its best she asks that the adults don't see her in her shrinking form. Now, come with me kiddos!" she said, and my feet began to follow her will. She told us that it would not take long. She led us up to her room. She wanted to tell us about how she longed to swap another gem for the emerald. I tried to walk away but was unsuccessful. As she pushed open the door, it looked like a regular bedroom with the lights switched off.

A sign read on the door handle read:
Please do not disturb. I value privacy.

Well, at least that made sense. Who knew what horrors that room would have? I saw Mira grabbing Jake's wrist so tight that her knuckles turned white. Nephia turned on the light, after checking that the door was locked firmly. But the light didn't illuminate the room. It cast a dim, red glow onto the horrors of the room. I could now see cobwebs hanging from the ceiling that were not there before. Black cloths were draped around the interior. Cages containing rattlesnakes, spiders (tarantulas mainly), crocodiles and wasps. They all had gleaming red eyes. Poisonous, black bats swooped from corner to corner, flying over a crooked, black sofa in the centre of the room. The carpet was patterned with distorted skulls. Skeletons were in an extremely dark cupboard with the doors ripped off. They were glowing faintly. Something dark red was dripping from a crack in the ceiling. I shivered. The temperature was low, and blood-red icicles were hanging from the ceilings. A rather gruesome looking chair was standing in the corner of the room. It was made entirely of bones and was glued together with something red and gloopy. Then, something caught my eye. I saw a little notebook, where someone had written down some notes. I looked closer. It read:

Dear Nephia, My dearest granddaughter,
Instruction Manual for room.
- *Always lock the door before turning on the lights.*
- *Make sure that the repelling potion is dripped carefully around the door every 24 hours in case any mortals come snooping. The potion will make the victim remember an important meeting with Mr Jacks and will rush off.*
- *Never scream or shriek spells while footsteps are outside the door. Remember Samra Hill's curse. Door flies open and light goes on.*
- *Remember I will come back soon.*
Hawk Everdark.

I was rather confused. I didn't understand. I knew that Samra Hills was my great grandfather; how could he curse something? He wasn't magical… or was he? If he could, which seemed likely enough, maybe I was slightly like him. Maybe a wee bit magical as well. If I could, maybe I could defeat Nephia… or do something that would make me famous!

I had experienced enough trouble for almost 2 days. I knew that this would continue for a week and if (sorry, I am finding it hard to say) and if Mira didn't survive, then for my whole life I would suffer the guilt. It would destroy me if she died. I hoped with my life that she would be okay. I knew that it sort of depended on me. And Jake. And Liam.

But I hated to admit, Nephia was stronger than any of us would ever be. *That letter gave me some hope.*

Every evening, my dad came to our room to call me for dinner. He would wait until 6:20 and if I didn't go down by 6:30, he would come up. It was now 6:29. I hoped that he would come knocking. I strained my ears to listen. Then, slowly, surely, my father's footsteps came closer and closer. I nudged Jake as Nephia stroked a skeleton's cold, hard fingers tenderly. I mimed yelling.

When Nephia finally focused on Mira, with a bottle in her hand, a wicked, gleaming grin on her face, Jake and I *screamed*. Nephia's eyes widened with hatred and put her ear to the door as my dad's footsteps got closer. The light switch was right next to her, and she immediately clamped her fist over it. Then she snarled, and she quickly shoved us angrily into a sofa that had magically appeared. A plate of scones appeared and parts of it rapidly began vanishing to make it look half eaten. She whispered to us murderously, "This isn't the end!". Suddenly, the TV got switched on. Just like that, the room had transformed and looked perfectly normal. She vanished and went to the other side of the door as it flew open.
"Mr Hills, what do I owe the pleasure to?" she asked sweetly.
"I was just wondering if you had seen my little Jadie. I came to collect her for dinner." said my dad.
"Ever so sorry. Jadie and her friends decided to come over for a cuppa. We were watching Television so didn't hear you." She told him.

We leapt out of the seat before the sofa could swallow us or something worse and leapt towards my dad, just as the clock read: 6:30.

"Mr Hills, do you fancy a cup of tea?" Nephia asked hastily.

"Ok..." My dad said as he stared at Mira. She looked uncomfortable. I watched carefully as Nephia made a cup of tea. I wouldn't have done it any differently. But then, I watched as she made a second cup of tea. I gasped as she put something blue into it.

Feeling a sense of dawning apprehension, I watched as Nephia passed it to my dad. I watched with held breath. Instead of crumpling to the ground choking or wheezing, he smiled contentedly.

Then, she passed me to give it to Mira. She whispered, "I swear this isn't poison however tempting it could be." It felt as though she was shoving the drink into Mira's mouth. Mira looked worried for a second, then, she narrowed her eyes and gave me a reassuring nod that meant: *It's fine.*

Mrs Smith AKA Nephia went to chat with my dad. Jake came up to me and said, "You know, do you think that you might have a magical power, you know, like Samra?". He continued in a joking manner, "Maybe you can fly, or control wind? Hahaha!" he laughed. Sparing him one look of disgust, I went to talk to Mira, but she was not in the mood for talking.

We quickly said goodbyes and made our way to dinner. We could not have been gladder to leave. Thank goodness my dad came to check on me.

When we reached the dining hall, Mira did not eat her delicious shepherd's pie, that lay waiting to be eaten. She was a sickly white and her mother was trying to feed her. Her mother's hair was matted and messy and she was rather upset. Mira hadn't been eating for two days. I was so glad that Mira had chosen that her mum would see her as before. Her mum would have been a lot more upset if she could see Mira in her cursed form!

Nephia also came to dinner. She walked by our table and stopped to look at Mira. Her red bag was inches away from my hand... Overcome by curiosity I looked into her bag.

Feelings.

I took the bottle out.

This potion makes the drinker feel any emotion that another person has. You have to say their name. Only for sadness or anger. It only lasts a few seconds. **DO NOT TRY TO USE FOR HAPPINESS OR JOY.** *(Or drinker will get blasted to pieces.)*

I knew that Mira was not feeling over the moon, so I knew I was quite safe. I dabbed a bit on my skin. "Er… Mira?" I asked the potion hesitantly.

For a moment, my friend smiled and began eating hungrily as my head felt heavy with grief.

So many feelings were spinning in my head, and I felt as if I was carrying the weight of the world on top of me. My muscles seared and burnt like fire and my heart was overcome with hopelessness and terror. I tried desperately to find some sort of hope inside me but found none.

Then, it was all over, the whole thing had happened in a flash. But that moment, I will never forget, no matter what I do, no matter what I see or where I am, I will remember that horrible feeling.

I had finally realised the terrible burden that my friend was carrying.

7. The strange man

It was over, as quick as lightning, she was looking pale and clammy again and stopped eating. My heart ached with sadness, and I stared sadly at Mira for several moments. I couldn't believe how Mira had managed to cover that up and bear with it. There were tears, big, sad tears welling up in my eyes.

"Are you ok dear?" my mum asked me in concern," You have gone red." She added. I blinked back the tears and nodded. I hadn't even realised that she had joined the table.

"Its just- actually, forget it mum. I'm fine." I said untruthfully. She raised her eyebrows. She asked again but I just couldn't say anymore.
"I'll talk to you later dear." She told me eventually.
"When does the museum open again?" I asked after a little while.

"Hmmm… maybe a month. You see, the door will not open because the pillar was knocked over and badly damaged. It will take about 2 weeks to put the pillar back into its place. They need to understand how it happened so they can fix it in a way that it won't break again. Then, another 2 weeks for double, maybe triple safety check. I still don't understand how a little boy tripping over can cause a big pillar to fall. Oh man, it is hard being the head of the hotel." She complained, watching my face crumple and the big frown of despair unfold on my mouth and eyes, "Oh, don't worry, soon, I will be investigating along with them, I will take you with me if I must." My eyes lit up.

"I don't know the proper timing, but soon." She promised.

"Before Saturday? I asked.

"Before Friday." She smiled. I grinned and linked my pinkie through hers, my first proper smile in days. The day Mira got cursed was on Monday, today was almost Wednesday. We had 4-ish days to help Mira. I was sure that we could make it.

Or at least I hoped.

"If this business troubles you so much, dear, you can watch the CCTV cameras. You have always been able to spot things that I don't." I felt better instantly and smiled.

Everything was going to be alright.

If my great grandfather could defeat Nephia, then I could too. As long as Nephia's grandfather did not come back as he had predicted, I thought that I would be alright.

My mum continued, "It is such a mystery, I don't know how the pillar could get damaged so easily. It's been there for years! Who else could have been there and caused all that damage? Oh, well, I guess that you might see something that I can't. You have always had sharper eyes." She told me grudgingly.

"Thanks! Bye!" I told her, my whole face lighting up suddenly, "Quick question, is it dark in the security room?" I asked.

"Well… yes. Quite dark. If the door is shut. And it is also quite dark in the video. It was about 8 o'clock at the time." She added with a trusting look. I rushed out of my seat and accidentally knocked some pasta onto the floor. I was about to tell Mira, but remembering what she was feeling, I went to Jake instead, as Liam wasn't there.

"Oi, I just got my food!" he complained as he followed me reluctantly. I took him to the security room and switched on all the lights. I triple locked the door and kept a torch in my hand.

No 'shadow walking'.

Jake turned on the screen quietly and we silently watched it. There was a small child with sandy hair and was dressed in red. He was admiring the pillar with fasciation as he ran his fingers over the sign which read:

This special pillar has come from the other side of the world! Mexico! It is a rare artifact, found buried inside the ancient ruins of a temple and...

Blah, blah blah. I saw that most of the people were crowding around 'The pillar that had come from out of space' and were reading the sign. It was rather dark in the video, and the clock showed 8:15. I wondered why the little boy was allowed to come at that time. The museum closed at 8:20 anyway. The little boy was probably in the darkest part of the room, and I noticed that his shoelace suddenly began to look slightly damp, with a hint of green mixed into the white. It was also unfolding itself. I bet no-one noticed that. Then, the video showed that the shoelaces were undone very clearly, and the boy was walking slowly towards the pillar. After that, he tripped over his laces and fell onto the pillar. The whole thing toppled over and broke into two, and I saw a rather shadowy hand cut the string within the pillar. The screen fizzed to black, and the little boy was left, staring into the shadows. I expected that Nephia pushed him into it. The screen did not show the top of the pillar that well. There was a lot going on in the video, but my eyes were fixed on the boy. I had a hunch that I should focus on his shoelaces as mum told me about him tripping up.

Jake's eyes were wide with excitement and mine were shining with fear. Hopefully, I would not have a troubled sleep dreaming about ghosts or something worse. I didn't want to know where this information would take us, but I knew that now, I was very glad to be in bright, warm light. Jake opened the door to let me through. For a split second, I saw a figure in a hooded cloak. Then, everything went black.

Suitcases. That's what I thought would be dealing with when my mum became Head of this hotel. Maybe a coat or two to hand back to forgetful guests. Never did I dream of having to face power-hungry and evil sorcerers who clearly wanted me dead. As I felt through the darkness, 5 long and cold fingers brushed against me and ran through my hair. "Hotel Srakolian. Hotel Srakolian. Hotel Srakolian." The walls seemed to whisper. I found Jake and together we switched on the torch. As the light switched on, we saw a cloaked figure stand there, caped in black and a grey hood covering his face. "96 years! Recovered from the underworld..." the voice croaked. It did not sound like Nephia's at all. It was a hoarse and rough voice, that does not sound like it belonged to the kind of person who would do any good to 2 frightened kids. "Who... are you?" I whimpered, trying to keep the squeak out of my voice. I heard Jake muttering prayers under his breath.

I was terrified. "Who am I, you ask?", in his mysterious and coarse voice. I shuddered: it felt like talking to a frog. "Missy, shouldn't you know the story? The story of a strange man coming to the hotel and asking you to change the name. Well, at that time, the Hills generation were not owners of the hotel yet. The strange man, whose name was Samra, told the owners to change the name to Hotel Saturn. The reason he did this was because the name of this building was like a magnet, attracting people like us. People who are called evil, by people like you! It took many months to finally persuade them to change the name. But when they did, it was far too late. And one of the so-called evil forces had managed to sneak in. Perhaps you know Nephia Everdark? My beautiful, charming granddaughter?" He left the silence ringing in the air. I knew that this must be Nephia's grandfather. Hawk Everdark. The silence gave me the chills.

"Your rather witty grandfather managed to find out that I'm one of the so-called-evil and kicked me out when they changed the name. So, you probably realise that I am Nephia's grandfather indeed. It has been 96 years since I first walked the very halls of this hotel. Oh yes. And when the then owners decided that it was enough, he became the head of the hotel and naturally your generation follows his lead. But before I was kicked out, I told my Nephia as many secrets of magic that I could remember. Oh, I never forgave old Samra!".

I stared at Nephia's grandfather as he told me that now that he had introduced himself, he would go to his granddaughter's room.

"She should know that her loving grandfather has now arrived. And for your sake, I shall tell you this. Should you ever try to destroy Nephia, you will never succeed, our powers are too strong."

And just like that, he disappeared into the darkness. I felt Jake slide down, unconscious, onto the floor beside me. There was a dull THUD that echoed in the room. I banged my fists onto the walls and tried to find the light switch. My mind was more focused on how we were to survive. Poor Mira, she had enough on her mind, and now, when I would tell her this piece of information, she might collapse of stress and worry. I was wondering if I should tell my mum when she opened the door.

"Oh Jadie, you poor thing? Are you alright? Oh, what on earth happened to him?" my mum screamed, running into the room. She checked that I was alright and gave my shoulders a squeeze. Then, she bent over Jake and checked him. She told me to go to bed. I quietly slipped away, my dad escorting me unwillingly. I could tell that he preferred to be downstairs. I told him after a while that he could go down, and without a second thought, he agreed. I thought about the skeletons in Nephia's room and wondered if one was Samra. If so, perhaps I could talk to him. He could give me advice, like Hawk had given Nephia. On the way, I saw Mira, walking sullenly towards her room. Her face was the colour of old porridge and her face had fingernail marks all over it. I tried to avert my eyes from her, but she recognised me immediately.

"Jadie! You idiot! Why on Earth didn't you take me to see the camera footages? Why Jadie? Just because I'm small and cursed! Why?! I could have helped!" she wailed furiously. I tried to back away gently, but she wasn't done yet.
"You are giving me a full explanation RIGHT NOW!" she shouted angrily.
"Yeah… so, we found Nephia's long lost grandfather, who was sort of resurrected from the dead, and then, well, I found out that my great grandfather is kind of magic, but I don't know everything yet, and we should be allowed to go to the museum tomorrow." I told her nervously. It was like watching a bomb, wating for it to explode or something worse. However, all she said was, "Great."

Then, she walked off, just like that. She looked very stroppy and moody and as she stormed off, I saw tears burning fiercely in her eyes. I felt immensely sorry for her and turned away slowly. I was surprised to be facing the door of my room so quickly, I was so carried away with my thoughts. Lucy was there, wrestling with the bathroom door as she hopped on the spot angrily.

"Oh, hey little girl." She told me as I slouched in, "Something bothered you?" she asked. She told me that she had already heard about everything.

Our room was massive, and far away from the others. Nephia's was opposite our annexe, her window facing ours. Our door was painted gleaming black and there were 4 bedrooms; 4 bathrooms, a gaming room, and a dining room as well as a nice TV, and plenty of cushions. We had a beautiful balcony that overlooked the beach. It was so blissful to watch the sun set and sit there eating marshmallows (that were toasted of course.) It was the perfect room for me. It took up plenty of space, though it was at the very top adjacent to the hotel. My mum's office was at the top of the hotel. Every day, we would walk through the gardens towards our private entrance.

I watched as she struggled in vain to pull open the bathroom door.

"Why are you pulling?" I asked her innocently, trying not to laugh as I watched her face turning red and trickling beads of sweat down its perspiring forehead.

"Don't you have to?" she asked, her voice becoming dangerously low.

"Um... no, you er have to push." I told her, my face turning pink with the effort not to giggle. She gave a huge groan that I swear could have been heard by my dad, still in the hotel. She flopped onto the carpeted floor, moaning and growling angrily. I stepped into the bathroom and closed the door hastily behind me, locking it, just as Lucy was about to open it. I buried my head into the towel and laughed until Lucy started to sob in desperation. I got out hastily and allowed her to go in. She gave me a punch in the gut, which I didn't blame her for.

Soon, my parents came, my mother's face white with worry and my dad talking rapidly to her,

"Poor boy, what will the parents think of us? It was only Jadie and him who were in that room! We must invite them around to your office, or something." He was saying.

"Yes, but surely, little Jadie wouldn't do such a thing. Jake and Jadie are friends! She wouldn't have done that! When the boy wakes up, I hope he tells his parents that our girl didn't do it." My mum was telling him anxiously. "Right?" she asked.

Then, she saw me, and her expression darkened for a moment.

"Jadie! You have to tell me everything! Right from the beginning young lady!" she told me severely. I gulped.

"Well, we watched the screen, and when it finished, the room went black, and Jake bumped his head on the wall. Then, he fainted." I invented. I was still thinking about how I suddenly had felt that flash, when I could read Mira's feelings. I wondered if Nephia had done that on purpose.

"You know, you were born with sharper eyes. It is not like something odd or weird. Its unique. Its special. Your great grandfather told us that you would have slightly sharper eyes. He had them too. Saw things other people didn't." my mum told me. I thought that it was a bit random of her to suddenly break the silence with that. I did feel better, cooler, a bit magical. That I was really someone who had genes from a sorcerer. I grinned for a moment, maybe 2.

"Well... Did you see anything interesting?" she asked. I could tell that she was bursting to ask this. I shook my head.

"Er... Jadie, are you feeling, ok?" my dad asked me nervously.

"Just tired, that's all, you know, all this weird business about Jake. I will go to bed." I told them firmly. They glanced at each other, uncertainly, but held my bedroom door open for me. I walked in slowly.

Immediately, I heard the lock click. My room is rather big, it has a dark shade of blue all around the walls, but you can hardly see them, my walls are covered from photographs of special events:

- The day we went to India with Mira
- The time when we built the museum
- The certificate that showed that my mum was Head of the museum
- A time when Jake and I were toasting marshmallows on a bonfire

Only to name a few

I expect that the archway and pillar will get added to the collection of hundreds of photos.

My bed was a double one where either the sunlight or moonlight would flood through the curtains, falling daintily onto my pillows. Currently the vast beams of moonlight slanted across the duvet like waves in the endless ocean. My bed was a hue of purple, dark green and shades of blue. I loved it. I had a massive, walk-in wardrobe. A bookshelf lay in the corner and my bedside table was groaning with the weight of the books. I took one of the volumes off the cabinet. It seemed to creak as if saying *"Oi! Take some more! I can't handle this burden!"*.

I started to flick through the pages of the book, eventually yawning and finally, deciding to go to sleep. I took out my secret cache of mints out of my bag and stuffed them into my mouth hungrily. I didn't have a lot of dinner. I snuggled down in my bed and fell asleep. I had a terrifying, horribly realistic dream:

I walked down the corridor to the breakfast room with Liam, when the smooth floor around us became lumpy and began moving about, causing us both to crash on the floor. Then, it began to feel wet, and I saw that the white marble was now a sickly green. But before we could rise (the lumpy, 'moving about' had stopped) the floorboards suddenly became like quicksand and eventually, we got sucked in. I thought that this would be the end of me. But it wasn't like the afterlife exactly. It was more like… The Museum?

I was terrified and rather cold. It was very dark. I saw a small figure come up to me with innocent, doleful eyes.

"Jadie!" Mira whispered. "I have got 2 minutes left to live. Nephia is guarding the stone, I can't get past! There is a weird dude with her!"

I gasped. We hurried to the emerald.

"Boo." snarled a voice from nearby. We almost jumped out of our skins.

"Good of you to join the party, we just got started." Hawk smiled evilly. Then, he began to tie us up with invisible bonds. I struggled helplessly. When he was finished, he said, "Your friend has got 20 seconds."

It felt more like 3. I felt Mira's trembling hand working on the ropes behind me…

"15 seconds!" he shouted.

I felt Liam brush against me writhing in agony and determination...

"Ten nine eight, seven, six!"

I felt a wave of despair crash over me. Mira clutched mine and Liam's wrists tightly.

"It -will -be -alright, - I'll -die- with- my -friends- fighting - beside-me." *Mira grunted in pain and desperation.*

"THREE, TWO -ONE!" *he yelled as a blinding flash surrounded Mira, until there was nothing left of her.*

I woke up, dripping in sweat, my hands cold and clammy. I looked in the mirror and saw a grey, scared face staring back at me.

"It is ok, just a dream." I whispered fiercely to myself. I realised that I had been screaming and shouting in my sleep. My bleary- eyed, parents came into my room, with concern in their eyes.

"You ok Jadie?" My dad asked me sleepily.

"Fine." I told him and quickly buried my head into the pillows. I pretended to snore, hoping that my parents wouldn't notice that my snoring was like... an octave lower than usual. They shrugged and slowly went away.

8. The big reveal

I went back to sleep and got a much better dream. One about the hotel getting attacked by these weird, walking jelly toys and me saving the hotel by blasting them all away. Then, I got some nice hot chocolate and pancakes.

I woke up, ready to face the day.

I got dressed and tied my hair rather untidily. I wanted to hurry down, but my mum made me make my bed and tie my hair properly. I hated it when I had to make my bed. I thought that it was a waste of time. I rapidly made it and rushed out before anyone could stop me. (They didn't bother to.) I tried to meet Mira on the way, but it seemed that she had ordered her breakfast to her room and wasn't ready to meet anyone yet. I hovered in front of her bedroom for a bit and then walked down.

By the time I made it to breakfast, my parents were already there. My dad was dressed in a business suit with a blue tuxedo and my mum was clad in a yellow and pink, smart dress.

"Where are you going?" I asked them curiously.

"3 things today. We are going to have a little interview to explain the reasons behind the tragic event in the museum. And then of course, speak to the young man's parents. Last of all, well, you know what that is." my mum whispered.

"What is it?" I asked, rather impatiently.

"The trip to the museum of course!" she told me, speaking normally again.

"Of course! I totally knew that!" I told her, smiling. But I felt terrified inside.

I didn't know what I would see in the museum. I tried not to think what would happen if one of us accidentally stepped under the archway. I tried not to show my look of worry to the others. It was day 4. We had 3 days left. I was starting to lose hope. Mira didn't even come down to breakfast today.

I spotted Jake and his family at a nearby table.
"Can Jake and I go and see Mira?" I whispered to my mum eagerly, still staring at Jake's family. She hesitated.
"Well, um… we will talk about it as soon as we finish our toast and omelette." She told me, avoiding Jake's parent's suspicious looks. When we finished, she dragged me by the wrist into the staff room outside the breakfast room. She ignored Mr Reynold's questions as she sat me down on a comfy stool.

"Jadie! What in the world is going on? Firstly, have you forgotten your manners?" she scolded, "You don't whisper into other people's ears in front of guests! And second and more importantly, you can't go anywhere with Jake alone, now that half the hotel thinks you knocked him out! His parents will refuse! And I can't do anything about that!" she told me firmly. I flinched.
"Look," she said, more softly this time, "Jadie if you could just explain everything to me…"
"No, I can't." I interrupted fiercely. She sighed.
"Fine, do you know what's happening?" she asked gently.
"No." I told her firmly. I didn't know all of it, I don't understand.

"Fine." She sighed and seemed to give up.

I walked out as quickly as I could, without running. I bumped into Jake's parents, who were talking quietly. I tried to slip away.

"Hmmpff. Jadie. Come back and look smart about it." Jake's father told me severely. I unwillingly came.

"Where are your parents?" he asked suspiciously. I nodded my head towards the room. Jake's parents walked over to the room and Jake's father knocked on the door in an impatient way. He was dressed smartly and told me briefly that he and Jake's mum were going to speak with my parents about what happened last night. My mum opened the door quickly. She waved Mr and Mrs White, (Jake's parents) to a velvety sofa. My dad came in soon after. He was shivering for some reason, but then, as it was said at the start, he always feels cold. They began to talk, and I slowly slipped away. I bumped into Jake. *How many people was I going to bump into this morning?*

"Hey! What are you doing?" he asked loudly.

"Jake! Reduce the *volume* a little bit!" I told him.

"Oops. Apologies. I have to explain how you didn't try to murder me last night. Bye!" he chuckled and went into the room.

I grimaced and went off. I was admiring the ancient picture when I heard an odd noise, coming from Mr Jack's study. I hesitated. If he caught me snooping, he was sure to send me to some sort of dodgy summer camp, 3000 miles away or more. But of course, curiosity got the better of me.

"Mira! What on earth are you doing here?" I shouted in surprise. She looked awful, her face slightly blue, fingernail marks all over it. She was wrapped in a blanket, shivering, as the sunlight was slowly giving her a tan.

"You don't know what it is like. Knowing that you are going to die in 3 days," She whispered hoarsely, "I have been looking for news. Anyway... you won't tell me anything." She added.

"What!" I cried, "I tell you everything!"
"Not yesterday you didn't. You went with Jake and didn't even tell me everything. I learnt what happened from my mum."

She shuddered, wincing as her toe came in contact with a soft piece of rubber. I decided to ignore this as I didn't want to tell her about how I had experienced her feelings yesterday.

Mr Jack's study was rather neat. Except the table. His table was covered with files and half of his newspapers were soaked with tea. I looked idly at the paper. My hands shook.

<u>Chaos again at Hotel Saturn.</u>

Inheriting the ancient building from her grandfather, Mrs. Julie Hills (42) has once again stirred some mystery in Shady Lane. Mrs Hills has had a rock fall into her house, coming from the sky, crashing into the mud heap. Not only that, but a few days ago, her rather dangerous hall, which she calls the museum, had a rather nasty accident inside those ancient rooms. A sarcophagus has tipped out its rather horrid contents and a vast pillar has toppled over of its own accord. The tragic events in Hotel Saturn are very disturbing and it is advised to not book any rooms in there. Residents recommend ignoring all vacancies. The council will inspect the hotel on Thursday, August 15th.

It appears that Mrs Hill's daughter, Jadie Hills (11) has knocked out a boy, Jake White (12) and has left both children's parents extremely confused. Mrs Julie Hills claims that her daughter would never do such a thing. Her husband, Paul Hills (45) been accused of cooking low-quality meals for the hotel guests. Mr Hills is the head Chef at Hotel Saturn and has made some peculiar meals. We have unconfirmed reports that another guest, Mira Partail (11) confined to her room. We are not entirely sure if Mr Hill's cooking is the reason for her absence. You might not know about Hotel Saturn's mysterious history. If not, go to page 8 to find out more about this hotel's past.

Skyla Brooks.

I looked, horror-struck at the piece of paper. Mira was reading another one, her knuckles white and she was finding it hard to hold the paper. I scowled angrily at the paper and mischievously poured the contents of the rest of Mr Jack's tea onto the paper. I realised a split-second later that I could have read more and found out what else this 'Skyla Brooks' was writing. This made me feel worse and I cursed angrily. I tried to make out the faint, blotted lines of ink, letters and tea but was unsuccessful. Mira looked over the top of the newspaper and sighed. She looked mournfully at me and averted her eyes miserably.

"You've no idea how I feel. It is much better knowing that-" she began softly.

"That your home will be destroyed by a couple of people who write the 'Daily news,'" I told her bitterly, "knowing that your home is displayed as some sort of freak building and this stupid Skyla Brooks is telling everyone that they shouldn't come to your hotel, and that you can't tell them the reason why this is happening, otherwise you will die."

Mira stayed silent for a moment. Then, her eyes lit up and she clapped her hands excitedly, not appearing to be affected by what I said.

"Jadie! I've got a brilliant idea! Well, hopefully we won't be able to use it but…"

"What is it, Mira?" I asked impatiently.

"If I don't survive, if the curse gets complete, you know, then maybe, say there are 5 seconds left, I could just tell them, I know that I would die…" she drifted off.

"NO! That is the most TERRIBLE, HORRIBLE, NOT HAPPENING IDEA!" I shouted, "Nope on a rope! We will save you." I added with certainty (sort of). She sighed sadly.

"Well, if that is the case, I don't know what we could do..." her momentary happiness evaporated, and she slumped down in despair.

"Haven't I told you?" I asked her suddenly, my memory coming back to me.

"Told me what?" she asked morosely, with not the slightest spark of interest.

"That we are going to the museum in roughly an hour." I said happily.

"What?" she shouted so loudly that the paper fell off the table as it rattled.

"Um, yeah…" I began.

"YES! YES! YES! YES!" she screamed so loudly that the birds outside fell off their nests.

Mira finally seemed her own self, smiling joyfully and jumping about, her face full of colour. Her cheeks were rosy and flushed and her eyes shone with glee.

She danced around the office, jumping on tables, kicking off valuable trophies, smashing Mr Jack's tea on the floor. She told me that this was the best thing she had heard in days. She was so hopeful; I knew that I couldn't let her down.

"When are we going?!" she squealed.

"Today, after the meeting and interview.

"What interview?" she asked, frowning slightly.

"Oh, one that my parents have to tell the community about the crazy things happening at the museum and reassure everyone." I told her.

"Good for your mum, she should show everyone that it wasn't her and that *that* idiotic woman is wrong." I was surprised that Mira would talk about Skyla like that, after all, she did read the paper every morning, after having her tea.

She skipped out of the office and took about a bathtub full of newspapers.

"Hello Madam!" she cried as soon as she saw the next person. I held my breath nervously.

"MIRA! You do not speak to your mother like that! I have never been a 'madam' to you! Though, I do like the poshness. You seem to have got a lot more cheerful." Mira's mother's voice came from behind the door. I cursed under my breath.

If Mira couldn't recognise her own mum at first sight, would she realise that she couldn't tell her mother about the curse?

I waited with bated breath.

"Oh no, nothing wrong, just, a lot happier, you know, I had an argument with Jake the other day and Liam and Jadie ganged up against me. That is why I didn't want to eat! Now, I have made up with them. All peace!" she lied.

"Ok, you should have told me dear!" her mum told her in a hurt way.

"Apologies." Mira said briskly and turned away. I grimaced. Her 'lying' skills were pretty good, but I was worried that her 'keeping secrets' skill wasn't. I followed her out of the room quietly. Before I left, I scanned the room quickly. I found a piece of paper that caught my eye. There, in front of my eye. There was a letter from Skyla to Mr Jacks.

Hiya Henry!

It has been a great summer, having a nice time? I know that it is so mysterious, everything about the hotel, your own manager is so suspicious! You may even be feeling like leaving! Well, don't worry, I will get rid of that lady. I will make her get sacked or fired or resign or whatever. No matter how, by spring equinox, that lady will be history. Have you heard about the interview? Just letting you know; Mrs Hills is having an interview with me in a few days. She has said that Jadie (her buffoon of a daughter) is going to come as well. It sucks! Well, see you later Henry! If I see you, I'll give you a little more information. Try to keep this letter away from prying eyes and awkward questions.

Bye for now H!
Your caring friend,
Skyla B!
P.S. Thanks ever so much for spying on her and giving me info! It has earned me 5000 pounds this week already! It is only Tuesday! The newspaper machines are literally exploding! We are going to hire some people to do it for us!

I was worried sick. If she was going to interview my mum, she could interview me. And Mira.

SHE WAS COMING TODAY!

I gave a look of hatred to the piece of paper, before I slipped it into my jumper pocket. Mira's mum was strutting off, just as I followed Mira into the corridor.

"Jadie! Mira! You're supposed to be waiting outside!" My mum told us angrily as she caught us sneaking away. We followed her to her office.

"Hey! I have got an idea!" Mira cried suddenly.

"What?" I asked," Is it completely mental?" I added.

"No! Well, there is a 25% chance that you would die..." she argued.

"Then, we are not doing it. Even if there is a 0.000001%

chance that I could die, NO! I don't want to die! Jake and Liam and you might die!" I snapped.

"Well, can't I at least tell you?" she asked. I sighed and nodded unwillingly.

"Great! So, we can tell your mum about the curse and tell her about Hawk! Not Nephia! Nephia only made you promise that you couldn't tell anyone about her! Also, she only made *you* promise, I will tell her everything." she said happily.

"No!" I spat.

"Ok… I will just ask your mum…" she ran ahead of me before I could stop her and asked my mum something inaudible.

"Of course, you can speak to me privately Mira! Don't be afraid to ask! Jadie, would you mind waiting outside my office door for a couple of seconds?" My mum said.

I was fully aware that my face looked murderously at Mira and that I looked like a red, swollen balloon.

She was trying hard not to grin and was looking at me with innocent, shining eyes.

"F.. F…Fine!" I growled, flashing my teeth like a wolf.

"Jadie! What did I speak to you about this morning! You are not a wolf, or a tiger or a crocodile! Mind your manners!" My mum shouted, rather shocked about my rude behaviour.

Mira smirked at me mischievously before turning away with my mum, grinning slightly.

I was **MAD.**

I was so worried for Mira, about the curse, and now, she tells my mum something that I swore on my life not to tell! I had been so worried, the whole reason we were doing this was for her! Not for anything else! Maybe my mum would tell Nephia, and Mira could have blamed me for it!

- My lips were curled
- My face was contorted in rage
- My jaw was clenched
- My teeth were bared
- My fists were shaking
- My forehead was sweaty

I WAS FURIOUS! Why couldn't Mira trust that I would save her!

I thought that my mum might resign, or faint, or not turn up for the interview and Skyla would get an excuse to write some trash. All these feelings were swirling in my head like a hurricane and nausea was rising in my throat like a volcano.

I couldn't bear it.

I rushed to the nearest bathroom and threw up neatly into the toilet. I was still experiencing hatred and revulsion towards Mira. I ran back to the door and pressed my ear to the keyhole. I hoped against hope that she went in to talk about something else.

"That- How is that possi- WHAT- that doesn't-" I heard my mum stammering. Then, I heard a scream. It was a shrill, petrified scream. And the voice was my mum's. I couldn't bear it. I barged into the room.

Oh my- Oh gosh- help-what..." My mum gasped, clutching her hands to her chest in terror. Her hand was holding Mira's cheeks while Mira looked apologetically at her. She had told the secret... yet she did not seem dead.

I started flailing around like a crazy girl. I took my emergency siren out of my pocket. I pressed the button and the horrible, screeching sound echoed around the room. Security guards (from the lookout area), and staff (from various corners of the hotel) rushed in, carrying hundreds of medical objects.

It had worked. I was overjoyed, angry, relieved, scared, happy and shocked. All those feeling made me a bit dizzy. I sat down on the floor.

"JADIE! I NEED TO HAVE A WORD WITH YOU THIS INSTANT!" My mum roared, scaring the life out of the staff members.

"We are not doing the trip to the museum. I need at least 5 months to think about this situation that we are in!" she continued furiously. I cowered behind a chair.

"We only have 3 days! Remember!" I whimpered timidly.

"WHAT? IS THERE SOMETHING ELSE THAT YOU FORGOT TO TELL ME MIRA PARTAIL?" she yelled, facing Mira angrily.

"Er just a few bits and bobs." She whispered in a small voice.

"Right. Staff, get me a cup of tea, 2 tablespoons of sugar and mix thoroughly for 45 seconds, PRECISE! Not one millisecond later! Or even one micro-millisecond later! Don't forget to heat the microwave to Medium Hot. NOW!" she bellowed to the ladies from the kitchen.

"Yes ma'am." The ladies said and turned away quickly. The other staff followed suit. Soon, we were left alone. I felt awkward and embarrassed.

"Well," she demanded, turning to face us. We flinched, "What is this *extra bit* that Jadie mentioned about 3 days!"

"Um... I have 3 days left until the curse is complete and I sort of... die." Mira declared.

"WHAT?" I will not have a person die! You might have wanted to mention that!" My mum said sarcastically and angrily.

"Yeah, I was about to, but then, well, you screamed." Mira nervously stuttered. My mum gave a little, embarrassed wince.

"So let me get this straight. I have got an evil witch in my hotel and her long-dead grandfather has come back to life. One of my guests has been cursed by an ancient archway and she will die in 3 days. And my grandfather is a wizard." My mum said, counting off all points on her fingers and ending up with the number 6.

"More or less." I replied.

"More or less? MORE OR LESS! I couldn't see this girl properly and now I can! She is tiny! She is cursed! It is all my fault! I got that archway from Tasmania! I shouldn't have, if I hadn't, none of this would have happened!" she shouted, gesturing at Mira.

"How can you see her, I thought that..." I began.

"Mira sort of closed her eyes for a moment and then I blinked. When I opened my eyes, she was small!" my mum told me, trying to describe the incident.

"I dunno, the potion... I sort of concentrated hard and then suddenly your mum could see me. The others still see me normally, right?" she asked. I shook my head, not knowing anything anymore. She told me that only I had seen her.

"Hmmm, this is sounding more and more unreal. Are sure that this wasn't a dream? Or a made-up story that you expect me to believe? You must swear that it is not." Mum asked sternly.

"I solemnly swear on the my life that this is no joke." She promised.

"Ok, my interview is coming up, but I will come to you as soon as possible. Before you go, please can you pop by the shop next door, Harold's hankies? I left some notes there yesterday. I have asked them to keep it in the private security room. I would send someone else, but I must have a meeting with all my staff. And then, it's the interview, but I can't turn up late." We accepted to run the errand. "Thank you." my mum said looking distracted.

She buried her face into a hanky, and I thought that she might need a new one. We could buy it on the way. While walking to the shop, we met Liam. Mira said she would walk in the woods, so Liam and I went to run the errand.

"Hey mate! Smashing to see ya!" Liam cried into the desolate shop, putting on a falsely American accent.

A row of freshly made, pristine handkerchiefs were assembled there, ready to be bought. I looked in longing at the blue, satin bandana which was decorated in a way to mimic the waves of the ocean. I wouldn't mind buying one myself. The rather pale, sweaty man behind the counter gave us a hasty grin and fumbled for his coffee.

"May I help ye'?" he asked in a gruff voice.
"Yeah mate! We just need to go to your private room and take a few bits of paper." Liam replied casually.
"EXCUSE ME! Ye ain't goin' into any of me private places mate!" He roared angrily.

"Um- sorry, have you heard about that terrible incident in Hotel Saturn?" Liam asked, eager to start a conversation and become friends with this short-tempered man. I elbowed him in the ribs. I didn't want him accidentally leaking secrets about our hotel. Unfortunately for Liam, I want the only one who was angry at him.

The man's face was literally exploding with anger and 'redness'.

"YEAH MATE! OH, I'VE HEARD ABOUT THAT ALL RIGHT! THE RUDDY LUNATICS ARE SAYING ME BRUVER'S SON DID IT! HE'D NEVER HURT A STUPID FLY! THIS IDIOTIC JULIE HILLS IS A COMPLETE DODO!" he shouted so loudly that Liam cowered behind me. I grimaced and stepped forwards.
"I apologise on *his* behalf. Ever so sorry." I apologised, lying through my teeth and gave him a charming, gleaming smile. I saw Liam give him the evil eye. I wanted to do that as well. He was insulting my mother! But I carried on calmly and said we were sent from the hotel to pick up a notebook that was left in the Security room.
"Well, ok. I will let you in… but show your identity! What are your names?" he asked, snarling, and narrowing his eyes.
"Well, this is our identity and we're both 11. My name is Hadie Jills, and this is Liam… Pest." I told him, hoping he was extremely gullible. Then, Liam did something very strange. He looked at the man and then at his waistcoat pocket, where his wallet was sticking out, and then outside the window, his eyes widening.

"Liam *Pest?* LIAM *PEST?* I think that you mean Liam *West!* I know the horrible boy! He was the one who bumped into me last week and I lost my beautiful CREDIT CARD in the drain! He should have seen that I was balancing it one my palm! My poor money! I am stuck in this terrible shop, trying to sell hankies to snotty-nosed customers! They never come! I have been speaking to the credit card company and trying to sort out a new card for me! Do you know how hard that is? OH, YOU NASTY BOY!"

He bellowed, charging at Liam like an angry rhinoceros. Liam jumped out of the way, and he tumbled to the ground.

"Couldn't you have ordered another one *Sir?*" Liam asked mockingly. He snarled, spitting and growling, rising from the floor.

"Liam- is this true?" I asked quietly. He looked at me shamefacedly.

"I was shopping at the markets the other day, and I asked this random boy if he could show me where the cakes were. He accidently pushed me, and I bumped into this *gentleman*. It was outside and the credit card that he was balancing fell into the manhole. It was an accident. There was nothing I could do to fetch the card. He asked me who I was, and I told him my name and ran off." He replied guiltily.

"Ok, cool story, can you apologise. We can then collect our things and leave!" I sighed. I ran towards the far end of the room. I passed that blue hankie and pulled it off the shelf. It read: 10 pounds now 6 pounds.

I threw a 5-pound note onto the shelf and carried on running. I reached the table where the notebook was, picked it up and ran.

The shop keeper tried to follow but Liam slammed the door. The shop keeper ran after us and shouted out, "Hey! Come back!". He was stronger and faster and would soon get us, no doubt.

This book was important to my mum, and I had to get it to her. Fast. He sprang after us, his teeth gnashing furiously. As we darted past the corner, I saw Mr Seaweed's old electric bike lying uselessly on the floor.

Would he mind?

I didn't feel like I had a choice. Either face the muscular, fierce man or borrow a motorbike. I was feeling a bit rebellious already and I knew how to ride a bike... I could drop it off at Mrs Seaweed's ice cream parlour nearby. I knew her very well as I spent half my time at her shop in the summer. I shrugged. One ride wouldn't hurt.

It turned out that it did.

"AHHHHHHHIIH!" Liam screamed loudly as he scratched himself on the wall. I blocked tons of traffic as I sped illegally through the narrow roads. I accidentally brushed him against the a lampost and caused him to yell in horror.

"When you're older... tell your family that you are the world's most TERRIBLE rider!" he shouted and clung onto my waist for dear life.

"Will do!" I said sheepishly.

I tried to remember my 'bike lesson' with dad. But I just got distracted from that memory and pressed the brakes a little too hard that poor Liam fell off the bike. He was nearly run over by a red car!

"AAAAAAHHHHHH!!!!!!!!!!!!!" he screamed, as he was trying cling on to the kerb. I jumped off the scooter and helped him to his feet. A police car halted in front of us.

"Stop where you are!" Constable Pearce shouted, his eyes piercing down at us. "What do you think you are doing children?" he yelled.

"We- er- he- I-" I stammered and tried not to look at the bike.

"Young missus! You and your boyfriend better tell us your names! Where do you live? Where are your parents!" he scolded.

"She's not- I'm not…" Liam began, looking at me and rolling his eyes at the policeman.

"I am Henry Jacks. I'm staying at Hotel Saturn, and it is on Shady Lane. My parents are Jenifer and Mark Jacks." Liam explained, nodding his head at me when he was done.

"I am Jean Wills and I live in Hotel Saturn. My parents are Charlotte and Harry Wills." I said, uncomfortably aware of all the eyes on me. I would be on the news at this rate.

"Well," the police began, sighing," Would you like a lift home?"

I beamed," Thank you so much Sam." I had read his badge: Constable Sam Pearce.

"Do not call me Sam. I am Constable Pearce." He said gruffly," Get in." Constable Pearce said they would arrange the return of the electric bike. He did not look pleased.

The car journey was awkward, and we were once threatened to be chucked out! Well, Liam really.

"If you suddenly go 'BOO' one more time, you will go home in handcuffs." He warned him. Liam gulped. Soon, we got home, and Liam rushed out before saying goodbye or thank you. I gave a little bow and followed him swiftly.

"Liam! What?" I asked him incredulously as we reached the lobby.

"Oh, I'm sorry! They are all ruddy well MAD! And I have no idea why I got dragged into this! I should have gone for a walk with Mira" Liam replied angrily, storming away. I sighed and followed him into the corridor.

"Why are you following me?" he asked abruptly.

"Er… Sorry. I'll leave you to your thoughts then…" I trailed off and walked away.

I was met by my mum. I handed her the notebook and was about to get started on our little adventure.

"Jadie! Where have you *been?* I need to tell you some important news!" she shouted, almost barrelling into me.

"What is it?" I asked, puzzled.

"This is it. I'm resigning."

9. TANTRUM

"WHAT?!" I roared. I couldn't believe it.

"Um- yes. First thing tomorrow morning." She replied guiltily.

"But you- THIS PLACE HAS BEEN OUR HOME FOR GENERATIONS... FOR CENTURIES!" I shouted deafeningly. She flinched.

"We are moving to India, where your grandparents live. Start packing dear." She replied softly, giving me a hug. I shook her hands away.

"Dad and I have thought this hard and this is what we must do. Even *you* hid the truth from me. Have you *seen* those newspaper reports?! That Skyla Brooks! Devil woman! Mrs Smith! We thought she was a kind old lady a... *demon!*" she complained with anger and resentment.

"But Mira! My friends! How will we save Mira? I'm the only one who can." I protested.

"I am sorry J-Hills. I have already spoken to Mira's mum. She deserves to know whatever I heard from her own daughter. I would have wanted the same if my daughter had gone to another adult for help. This is the time to look after our own families. Yes, Mira's mum was shocked, angry. Everything you can imagine. But she is smart and capable and will find a way out. I have told her she can have anything and any help from the hotel and staff. We must do what is best for our family. We must do this for the greater good. I can't explain any more than this." She insisted sadly. J-Hills is what she calls me when she is either super sad or mega happy.

I couldn't think properly. My mind was boggled. I tried desperately to negotiate but in vain.

"But- are you at least taking the things in the museum?" I asked, raising my eyebrows.

"With a cursed object inside?! No, I am burning it. I don't know what else could be hidden." She replied sadly. I thought of the stone pillar with the emerald.

"NO! But what about the other stuff? They're not cursed!" I pleaded.

"Jadie, who knows what else is there. The only way you find out something is testing it. I'm not testing any more people on my relics. I can't have another one cursed like your poor friend Mira." She told me miserably. My eyes started to water, and my nose started to prickle.

"The hotel?" I managed to say.

"Oh, we'll make it a care home. It can be of use to those who need it." She replied. I knew that those intentions were good and if it were me, I would have burnt the whole thing down, but I still felt angry and bitter.

"Fine. I'll start packing. I guess I don't have a choice." I said and stormed off.

I cried to myself as I got my 2 massive suitcases down from the attic. One was a beautiful shade of crimson, and the other was a hue of blue. I liked them quite a lot but now I hated them. Wiping the tears off my cheeks, I emptied my whole drawer of dresses and T-shirts into the blue one.

Then, I put all my jeans and leggings and everything else into the same suitcase. I packed all my toys, games, teddies, books, and my phone. I winced as I put them all away into the other suitcase. My purse lay at the bottom. Mira's birthday gift, the survivor bracelet, lay wrapped up in a pair of gloves. I fingered it gently as I put it away. Then, I couldn't bear it any longer.

I wiped my eyes with a lace handkerchief and sniffed softly. I sat there in silence, for 30 minutes, unaware that I was late for my mum's announcement to the hotel and the interview in the museum.

My dad came and patted my shoulder. "I'm so sorry that this is happening Jadie! I know it's hard to move to the other side of the world! And leave your friends behind. But your mother has explained, and you must understand that it's for the best. I'm sorry. I'll explain more when you are perhaps older." He said weakly, giving me a hug.

"But- do you know about Mira?' I asked cautiously.

"What about her?" he asked.

"Er… she does not like-" I lied.

"My food? Oh Jadie! I don't care what Skyla Brooks says! Mira doesn't eat her own mother's homemade food! In the hotel or not!" he said earnestly, believing my lies. That made me fell a lot worse lying to him. I was tired and didn't have the heart to face my friends.

"Ok. Can I just eat here instead of downstairs?" I asked bitterly.

"Sure dear, I understand. Do you mind if Lucy comes and sits with you?" he asked. I shook my head and shrugged.

"That's my girl!" he smiled and gave my hair a ruffle before walking downstairs.

A fierce battle was going on in my head.

Mum has decided that we are leaving! What do I do? This is so unfair. I don't want to leave Mira. What will my friends do? Nephia could kill them. I must help them. I do not want to move to India and abandon them.

Well, what would you have done?

I sighed and waited for Lucy to come and get me my food.

"Hey sis! Tricky situations huh? I've always thought mum was a bit of a lunatic." She said, sitting down. I didn't bother to reply or even protect mum. I twiddled with my thumbs as she lay my plate of curry in front of me. I slowly ate, shuddering at each mouthful, trying to push it away. But Lucy wouldn't let me.

"Now Jadie, somebody lovingly cooked that food for you! They put their time, effort, and love into their work. They would be so pleased for you to eat it! Some people don't even get food!" she scolded.

I knew that she was being wise (for once) and that what she said was perfectly true, but I still felt queasy. I ate it quickly and immediately ran to the bathroom. I perched myself on the rim of the bathtub and gave a small, frustrated groan. After a while, Lucy knocked on the door.

"JADIE! OPEN UP! I REALLY NEED THE LOO!" she shouted from outside. I grimaced and opened the door. She ran straight past me slammed the door, cringing like a 2-year-old. For a second, a small smile unfolded on the edges of my mouth. But I was soon back to feeling terrible and teary.

"Oh... you're crying. Um, well... er, don't cry... ok?" Lucy said as she came out the toilet, fastening the strings on her jumper. I averted my eyes from her and stared at the one thing that remained on the sofa.

A glowing wristband that Mira and I had made when we were out at the beach 2 years ago. We were only nine at the time.

Mira had bought these cool, glowing twin wristbands that would only glow if it could sense the other's presence.

Mine would glow a deep shade of coral blue while hers would gleam a magnificent shade of jade. I fastened it around my wrist and collapsed on the sofa.

"Look J, I know all about this weird keeping-quiet business. I know that there is something inside you that you ain't telling no one." She said gently," I know that there is something you and yer friends know that mum doesn't. And there is something that you're forgetting." She told me wisely, nodding her head. I wasn't even sure that there was anything.

Then, it dawned on me.
I had to tell mum. I sprang off the bed as if I had been electrocuted and raced downstairs, knocking over Lucy's delicious plate of trifle.
"Hey! Jadie!" she shouted, nursing her pudding tenderly," You found what you needed?"

"Oh, I sure have all right." I muttered under my breath and dashed off to the vast, marble hall, where we were having the most important meeting of all. I saw my mum standing on a raised platform, looking sincere, yet speaking in plain, melancholic tones.

"-although running this magnificent institution for 15 years, I feel that it is right to step down and give this place to the homeless. It has been my greatest *pleasure,*" she said that word as if it gave a bad taste in her mouth. She also looked at Nephia while doing that, "-to house you all. I am extremely sorry that from this moment onwards, I am no longer the head of this hotel." She brandished a resignation letter and showed the crowd her signature, "I hope that this ancient building will be…"

"Mum!" I shouted running up to her from the back of the room. I was conscious of thousands of eyes staring at me with disapproval.

Two of them were my mother's.

"Not now dear! Go to you room *now.*" She scolded, glaring at me fiercely. I saw Nephia smirk in the crowd and give me a sneer. I curled my lip menacingly and gave a growl. I looked at my mum hard for one second before walking off, red-faced and cursing at Nephia and my mum. I waited outside the doors until a flood of bustling, chatting people gossiped about my mother. Nephia came out last. She had a small hawk sitting on top of her shoulder.

"He wasn't called Hawk for no reason." She whispered and snuck off. I skulked off miserably. I stabbed moodily at the bench as I perched on top of it.

"You, OK?" a voice came from nearby. I looked around. Liam West stood there, leaning against the sofa in ease. He had combed his hair in an odd fashion and was smelling suspiciously of chlorine, "Went swimming." He shrugged.

"As a matter of fact, I am NOT 'ok'." I snapped and refused to meet his eyes. "After all that has been shared with my mum and the other grown-ups, I just realised that I haven't said anything about the pillar. I came rushing to tell and didn't realise she was in the middle of something important. Now, she won't hear me, and I didn't know what to do. I need to tell her soon as possible about the pillar. Mira is dying! That is the only hope of magic that is keeping me going. We need to get there!" I told him angrily.

"I can't join you Jadie. Now that our parents know everything, we just must let them handle it. We will be grounded if they think we are still sneaking behind their backs."

"I guess you're right Liam… but how can I go away to India? How will I stay in contact? I can't go on my own and let you all face evil!" I cried, wiping my eyes bitterly.

"Number 1, We will write and call you every day. Number 2, You are strong. We will meet again." He nodded wisely. I wanted to believe him. I really did.

I knew in my heart that we would beat Nephia and Hawk one day. But my heart and spirit were broken. The last few days of terror had weakened my strength. I felt that mum was being selfish and so was I, in a way. Mira was about to die. What could 4 kids do against 2 fully-grown sorcerers? Her life relied and depended on her friends. But how could I stay back with them when my family had made plans to go so far away?

I wondered what Jake and Mira might be doing. Probably asleep or worrying themselves out of their minds. I heard someone call Liam's name in the distance. Liam gave me a swift squeeze around the shoulders and hurried off.
I stood there, staring into thin air, as his footsteps faded away.

10. Goodbyes

I could have stayed there all night, lost in my thoughts. *2 days.* I thought sullenly as my dad came in.

"Hey! J-Hills!" my dad said brightly, slapping me on the back. Hard.

"Ow!" I complained and firmly turned my back on him.

"Hey, Jadie! It is all gonna turn out well. I promise." He said in soothing tones and was trying to make me face him. I gave a snort. *Turn out well? The museum was getting destroyed tomorrow.*

He sighed and gave me a hug before going back to the kitchen. Three visitors trying to cheer me up. I just couldn't listen to any of them.

Footsteps.

This time, my heart leapt for joy and the colour flooded back to my face. A wave of emotion hit me in the chest, and I flushed.

"Hey." Mira said gloomily, coming and sitting next to me and resting her head on my shoulder, "It is all so confused and messed up." I noticed that she was wearing her wristband too and it was gleaming like an emerald.

"Even if you're on the other side of the world, so what? I know that we will meet again. You may be gone from sight, but not from our hearts. At the end of every dark tunnel, there is light. Bright, cheerful light. We have something worth fighting for. Something that Nephia will never *ever* have. Friends. We will defeat Nephia and Hawk in some way or another. I promise. I know it hasn't gone your way. I told your mum and she's told mine. I'm *actually* happier now and I hope you can be too." She said, wisely.

"Jadie, there's something else-" she began. The door flew open, and my mum stood, hands on hips and she was glaring at us.

"Mira, would you mind heading back to your room? It is Jadie's bedtime. I want to have a private chat with her." She said rather brusquely.

Even Mira didn't dare to disobey her. She could tell by my mum's stormy expression. She left quietly.

There is hope. We must battle on, for friends and for the goodness of the world.

I told myself, new hope flaring in my heart. I sighed and knew that I was in deep trouble. I waited.

"I'm sorry." That was not what I was expecting.
"What?" I asked uncertainly, thinking that my ears weren't working properly. She sighed. My mum held my hand and put her arm around me. I still didn't believe what my ears were telling me.
"I'm sorry. All of this. I just dropped the news on you 'Right we are moving to another continent and leaving all your friends behind.' I don't want to do this either, but I feel that this is right for us as a family. Don't you now feel the same?" she asked. I hesitated.
"I guess." I admitted after a moment.
"That's good. We will talk about it on the plane. I have a lot of documents and certificates to sign. Pip pip dearie!" she said and ushered me to the bedroom.

Well, what was left of it. The bed was gone. Lost in the lost. I got a sleeping bag and lay down. I refused to close my eyes as they leaked. I sniffled and huddled into my blanket. Even though it was a hot day, I felt shivers down my spine, and I shuddered. Then, I remembered.

"The pillar- I need to tell mum!" I shouted in a blaze of confusion. I sprang out of the bed and found myself facing several unknown people who were sitting on small, plastic chairs.

"Wha..." I shook my head.

"So, the password for that link Mrs Hills is 24768. No, that one, the big red button. Yes... now sign there, on that sheet of paper and take a photo. Here's my phone. Yes, now upload it onto the website here. Yes-read it all. Correct Mrs Hills... now..." a bald, gangly man was instructing her. He was wearing a smart suit and was straightening his tie while pointing to various parts of my mum's computer.

"What are you doing? Get out!" I yelled, stepping into blinding light.

"I am guessing that this is little Jadie?" the man asked my mum, who was perched on the sofa looking mortified.

"Now, Jadie Wadie! So good to see you! Want to go back to sleepy weepy! You are very limpy wimpy! So brave!" a rather dumpy woman with a sweet face said, walking up to me and giving me a warm smile," Mumsy is just going to sign a few deedy weedies!" she told me and rubbed my cold, clammy hand in hers. I looked at my mum, asking silent questions but the look on her face was clear: *Later.*

I scowled and turned. *Why did someone always stop me when I needed to say something important?*

I went back. I lay in my bed, banging my fist against a teddy and wishing that either that strange woman, Nephia or Hawk's face could be underneath my knuckles.

That idea seemed to get me to sleep. I had a troubled sleep. I woke up to the sounds of chirping from birds. Probably the last time I would ever hear these very birds. I sniffed and wiped my nose. I tripped over the hem of my nightgown as I shuffled to my wardrobe before realising that it was empty.

This was the last day.

I felt sickened. A wave of nausea bubbled up my throat and I rushed off to the bathroom. I threw up neatly into the toilet and felt instantly better. I took a small sip of my water bottle and looked around for my parents. The group of people had gone from last night (yippee) but I heard Lucy snoring loudly in her airbed. I heard my mum shouting from downstairs as she was probably trying to calm down a lot of angry people. I heard her running up the stairs and I imagined the staff chasing her. I felt bad for her. And for me too of course.

Was I, my mum's daughter going to sulk just because I had to step out my comfort zone? It wasn't her fault.

I sighed and scrambled out of my night gown. I wore fresh clothes and got my 'plane-trainers' out of a bag. I slung my backpack over my shoulders and hitched up my jeans. I wore the wristband and slipped a picture of me, Mira, Jake, and Liam grinning at the beach into my pocket. I sniffed and headed downstairs sadly. As I walked through the corridors, I thought that this might be my last time I would ever do that. My head was still spinning. I took the elevators downstairs by myself, having plenty of time to dwell on my miserable thoughts. I thought about all the visits from my friends and family. I thought about how they had comforted me. But they had no idea how I was feeling. I slipped my hands deep inside my jersey pockets and felt it's soft fabric. My eyes began to leak again as I sat down alone on the wooden table of the dining room. I looked around and saw everyone whispering and pointing and speaking in hushed tones. I saw Mira and Jake, whose families had decided to sit together, give me a grim nod. I gave a small whimper. I knew I couldn't join them.

"Harsh times kid." A voice came from nearby. I looked round and saw a man with sunglasses staring at me.

"Hawk!" I cried.

"That's right kid."

"This whole thing is because of you and your stupid granddaughter!" I complained.

"*Never* call Nephia stupid. And even if she is, what does that make you?" he asked smugly.

"I-Er..." I stammered.

"Ha, got you back kid." He smiled and went to sit with Nephia. I glowered at them.

My pancakes and syrup didn't taste that good and I ignored my strawberry milkshake. I looked around at all the guests. This was the last time I would probably ever see them. This was the last time they'd see me. The buzz of talk went to silence as my mum stepped into the room. She was wearing a beige overcoat and avoided everyone's searching eyes.

"Good morning darling." She told me quietly as two armed security men marched past. I winced and looked over at Jake and Mira's table. They hastily looked away. I felt strangely glad that my friends were ignoring me. My mum cleared her throat. I looked at her. She duly began to talk to me quietly.

"So, you ready for the big flight? Dad's speaking to Uncle Sam and then we should be ready to go. Except for the fact that Lucy is still asleep." She told me, stabbing bitterly at her bowl of porridge.

I told her in a low voice," Mum, Nephia and Hawk are over there. And one more thing…"

"Yes?" she asked.

"Well, there is this magical, green diamond in the museum and-" I began.

"Green? In the museum? Oh, my goodness, I am 100% burning that place down!" she said and looked alarmed. I could have kicked myself.

My mum SERIOUSLY LOATHES the colour green. She is *very* superstitious. She once painted a pencil green and took it to school when she was little. That day, everything went wrong. She failed her tests, had arguments with friends and much worse things. She HATES green. She always uses red things as green is the opposite colour to red.

I used to tell her that the theory was ridiculous, but I could understand now. I felt sorry for her.

"I am sorry mum, but…" I started to say.

"No buts. No matter if that is good or bad; we are not keeping a *green* object in our house. Never!" she said and refused to talk.

I felt so angry with myself. I felt that she was being *stupid*. I contorted my face to a scowl and curled my lip when anyone looked at me. (Which was every 2 seconds.) I huffed and bent low on my food. I could see almost every hole in my pancake. I took a pot of Nutella and began dipping the knife in and applying more and more to my pancake. I was so absent minded that I didn't realise how much I had put.

"Jadie! You have used all the jar! You are not eating that! Put some in this bowl!" my mum scolded after she had seen what I was doing.

I scraped off the dozen layers of Nutella and put it into a bowl. There was hardly anything on my food. My mum looked harassed and red-faced as she checked her phone, "Drink your smoothie. Dad says that Lucy has already had breakfast in bed. Come on, we are going. Come *now*." I knew that there was no point arguing so I drank my smoothie quickly and snatched a cookie from the snack bar. As it lay in my sweating hand, it began to change, taking form of a fortune cookie.

"Wha…" I began.

You shall never see your friends. You are doomed. Accept the truth. Mira won't survive. It read.

I glared in the direction of Hawk.
He mouthed: *ha-ha*. I was furious. I dropped the cookie and stamped on it.

"Stupid people." I muttered and snarled at him. I followed my mum out and was drenched in bright light. Our Audi Q5 stood there, shining proudly. We stood there for a while, and I wondered what we were waiting for. My dad, uncle, mum, and sister were waiting with me.

"We are waiting for the goodbye ceremony." Lucy told me as if reading my thoughts. She nodded to a bunch of flowers and slipped her hand in mine.

Slowly, people started to come out of the building. Some looked downright furious while some sobbed uncontrollably. Mira, Jake, and Liam's family came first. Mira flung her arms around me and pressed something into my hand. I saw that it was the pebble I rescued from the drain. I smiled. I looked at her mum, but she looked away.

"We will miss you," Mira whispered, "always." I could feel my eyes watering. Liam gave me a hug and Jake preferred to shake my hand. I would miss them *so* much. I brushed my eye and sniffed.

I waited for them to say goodbye.

"We're not saying goodbyes," Mira said, grinning toothily, "because we'll be seeing ya sooner than you expect." As if reading my thoughts.

I smiled. I wanted to believe her.

"Jadie," my mum said from behind, "We have to do the burning." I nodded and slipped Mira's hand in mine. We walked to the museum. My mum had arranged for the fire service to tend to it. I don't know how she manages to get people to do these kinds of things. What all did she tell them? I watched in horror as the firemen started bringing it down.

"Noooooooooooooooooooo!"

I yelled over the roar of the fire. I watched the flames wolfing down my favourite section of the building and dancing mockingly us.

Next to me, a pang of realisation hit Mira hard. I knew what she was thinking. She sank to the ground, tears streaming down her face, her once happy, sweet eyes were gaunt and looking at me in something beyond sadness. Her last hope of the emerald was gone. I couldn't help but collapse. My knees buckled and I fell. My mum caught me and held Mira and me tight.

I shook out of her embrace and ran inside before anyone could stop me.

I knew that it was an EXTREMELY stupid idea, but my brain was fuzzy, and I couldn't think straight.

I was mad.

I leapt about, avoiding the flames and inhaling fumes of horrid smoke. I choked as I ran and ran, until I reached the pillar. The light radiating from the green emerald was blinding. It kept away the fire somehow and burned brighter than ever. I watched as the stone archway crumbled to dust and all that was left was ash. Well, since that was done… couldn't the fire go out? Then, a face, a ghostly, grey face seeped out from the flames.

"Who…" I mumbled, momentarily frozen.

"Jadie, my great granddaughter, my sweet great granddaughter, you're so brave. Go, go before it's too late. Now! This is not safe! I'll keep the fire away from you, but it won't last! Quick!" the ghost said. I stared, incredulous.

"Samra." I breathed.

"Yes dear, now go. Go darling, go!" he shouted over the roar of the flames, "I died in fire, I return a ghost in fire, go!" he told me. I knew that Samra had died in a forest fire. He had innocently gone with Hawk and had ended up dying. (Such a coincidence.)

"How are you here?" I asked.

"No time! Go! I am melting. The pillar, I cannot do anything-"

"Can't do anything? You're a wizard for heaven's sake!" I screamed. I felt so angry with him. I wished the flames would swallow him up.

"Jadie? Go!" he shouted before he disappeared. I was alone. I stared at the pillar. I grimaced and tried to pick it up. I was already weak, with fire damaging my lungs, but I managed to shift it to an ancient tree that stood outside the gates. I wasn't sure how I managed to shift it. Maybe it was because emotion was pulsing through my body so hard. Maybe it was because Samra had given me some sort of magical power. Or maybe it was just because there was a perfect hole to hide it that was only about 2 metres away. I shoved it into the hole and stood back quickly. The tree suddenly shrivelled up and covered the hole. Perfect. I gave one last look at the hole, before scurrying away back to my mum. She was sobbing hysterically by the time I got there.

"JADIE! YOU COULD HAVE DIED! YOU WILL NEVER EVER DO THAT AGAIN! DO YOU UNDERSTAND, YOU DISOBEDIENT CHILD? ONCE WE GET TO INDIA, YOU'RE GROUNDED FOR 2 MONTHS AND…" she broke into tears again. I felt very guilty.

"I am sorry..." I apologised.

"Doesn't matter. Get into the car." She muttered, wiping tears off her eyes. I gave the three of them one last hug each, and traipsed sadly to the car. I looked back at the museum, which was crumbling to ashes. I thought about Samra, who had visited me. I sighed. I didn't seem so shocked now. I watched Mira outside bury her head in her knees. She was sat on the floor, weeping helplessly. She was the size of a barbie doll and was hard to spot. Luckily, she could still control who would see her true size. Liam's eyes were watering slightly, and I saw Jake ask him something and point to his eyes. I know for sure Liam said, "They are sweating man, of the heat."

I buried my face in my hands and sniffed. I opened my shoulder bag and took out a piece of chewing gum. I chewed it anxiously.

This is all Mira's fault. If she hadn't told mum, I would be eating my pancakes cheerfully, sitting next to Mira and chatting happily. And planning how to bring her back to her normal size.

And then, a better voice spoke in my head: *It wasn't her fault. She had done what she thought was right.*

I shook my head.

And then I remembered Samra. I was still shaken by my meeting with Samra.

Then, I had an idea. I reached into the front seat of the car and opened my handbag. I groped inside and pulled out a notebook with a pen bound to a leather strap. I took out the pen and ripped off a sheet from the notebook. I scribbled quickly.

Mira,

I am so sorry about all this. I will try to believe you, I promise. We will hopefully meet again.

Listen, important info. Go to the tree which blooms those nice apples by the side of the museum. Or what's left of it.

See the burnt tree? Dig around it as deep as you can. The pillar is inside. Please hurry. This may be the only way to save you. The gem is inside.

Jadie.

I stared at the letter uncertainly and hesitated. I folded so it could fly easily. Then, I yelled Mira's name and threw it into the air. Mira, startled and confused, grabbed it, and read it swiftly. She nodded at me and showed Jake. Jake grabbed the letter and disappeared through the crowd to find Liam. I gave a weak smile despite of myself. I looked at the hotel one last time before my parents and sister got into the car, gave a wave, and drove off, leaving everything behind us.

11. On the plane

It was a long trip to the airport. Partially because there was silence in the car. I couldn't complain as that was the way I wanted it to be. It gave me plenty of time to think. Mira's parting smile was stuck in my mind and so were Jake's and Liam's. I would have cheered up slightly if Nephia's jubilant grin hadn't joined theirs.

I hoped that Mira would have found the bush and was healing rapidly. Sweat broke out over my forehead as the airport came into view. We dragged our suitcases out of the car and ignored all the whispering around us. I watched as my dad dropped off the suitcases and talked impatiently with the man behind the counter.

I sighed. This was taking forever. As soon as my dad finished, we went to the shopping centre and walked around the marble corridors of the shops. I bought 12 envelopes, which were in 3 packs, and got a new fountain pen. Lucy bought a new gaming console and got herself 3 boxes of chocolates.

"Before you ask- they are only for me." She warned and picked up a bottle of Coke from the shelf.
"Lucy! Put that down! You are not *drinking* fizzy drinks! No, I am sorry- no listen Lucy! You are- please put that down- yes- you are not drinking Coke. NO, don't take that bottle of sparkling lemonade instead." Mum said, as she wrestled the bottle off Lucy. Lucy grunted and put it away, before strolling to another shop.
"Paul- please see what she is buying." My mum said, watching my dad lumber off to Lucy's retreating figure.

"Would you like a new phone case Jadie?" she asked as she held up a phone case, which she had picked from the shelf. It was a mix of green and blue and got darker towards the edge. I glanced at it.

"Sure." I said absent-mindedly. She went to the till.

I grimaced as the audio said that it was time for our flight.

"Good gracious!" my mum squealed and hurried out of the shop, half-dragging me with her. We went through that machine that scans you to make sure that you don't have any dangerous possessions. We didn't (obviously).

They scanned all our items and let us go.

We boarded the plane, and once again I felt a wave of nausea sweep through my throat. I took out the paper bag from the basket in front of me and almost threw up inside. We watched as my country, my dear England slowly disappeared below the clouds. I felt sickened.

I hoped that Mira would be back to normal soon. Would she have found it by now?

Then, a thought hit me. A horrible, terrible thought struck me. I rolled over onto my side and tried to breathe. I couldn't. Turning pale and my eyes wide, I started to squeeze my jacket that I had thrown off.

"Um- Jadie? J-Hills? You okay?" my dad asked me. I managed to shake my head.

"What happened?" he asked, extremely concerned, "Julie! Jadie has gone pale! Could you come please?" he shouted to my mum. She rushed over.

"Jadie? Are you hurt?" she asked. I shook my head vigorously. She read from my eyes: *Mira. Trouble. Curse.*

Her eyes grew wide, "Paul, may you sit with Lucy? I'll take care of Jadie."

He nodded and went to sit with Lucy.

"So? What has happened?" she asked.

"The pillar- never got a chance to explain- Samra- save Mira- Stop-stay the same." I panted, surprised to be able to talk.

"Er- in a way that I could understand." She asked impatiently.

"Well, in the museum, there was a pillar… and that pillar had a gem. and that gem could stop Mira's curse. But when you burnt it down…"

She looked horrified, "There is no other way to help Mira! Oh…"

"No, when I went inside when it was burning, Samra's ghost came and talked to me. He just advised me to get out. He returns in fire. Mama, it was so creepy!" I told her.

She looked shaken. "My grandfather. He came back?" she looked incredulous. She covered her mouth with her hands and stared at me, discombobulated. "Really? Dear Samra? My darling grandfather alive? A ghost?" she looked ready to faint on me.

"I know that is weird mum, but the most horrible bit is that the archway read: This gem will stop the curse of the ancient archway. It never said that the victim would go back to normal! And I didn't realise until now that Mira would stop shrinking when she finds the gem, but what if she never goes back to her old size?!" I cried, spilling out the terrible burden that lay in my heart.

She stared at me, thunderstruck.

"No." she whispered. "This can't be possible!" she croaked, her voice barely more than a whisper. "But Jadie, the pillar burnt, right?"

I shook my head and sighed moodily. She looked aghast.

"*No?* where is it? Tell me Jadie!" she cried, jumping up slightly.

"The tree. The apple one. In the hole beside that tree." I replied quietly. She looked overjoyed.

"Jadie! This is amazing! We have hope. Even if we are not there to fetch it, others can. I'll let them know soon as possible." she said.

She turned to me. "My staff, rather some members of my old staff are very trustworthy. They will find the pillar by dinner time. Let's at least have it in our hands and then see what use we can make of it. Now darling, go to sleep." She said softly. I looked at the piece of paper in her hand. She has someone to call, and I felt relieved.

For some reason, a warning flashed in my mind, and I knew at once that something was wrong. Something caught my eye.

I gripped the armrests of my seat and looked out of the window in wonder and terror. I saw a small, black hawk dive close to the window as it soared up. I gasped. The hawk turned one eye to me, and I saw an evil, malicious wink in them. Hawk Everdark.

12. We land

"That's not…" my mum stammered as we were in the skies. Then, the audio speakers began to speak.

"The plane will be landing in 30 minutes. Please fasten your seatbelts." Came a cool, female voice.

An airhostess came around and checked that we had our seatbelts on.

"Are there supposed to be all those birds?" I asked her, noticing about a dozen more join him, as if he was their leader.
"Funny you ask. Mr Richards says that it is a hawk but is obviously mistaken. Sorry I can't tell you more Miss, I can't go round spilling the captain's mad ideas, can I?" she chuckled. I smiled back. As soon as she left, I gaped at my mum.
"It is a Hawk! Hawk Everdark!" I almost shouted.
"I know." She looked worried. I was about to have a panic attack. I slumped down and looked downcast. She looked helplessly around.
"What do we?" I asked helplessly.
"I don't know!" she said and looked as if she was debating whether to jump out the window or not.
I tried to keep my eyes open, but I couldn't. I slipped off to sleep. I must have been VERY tired.

"Jadie! We've arrived!" I heard a voice say.
"Mum? What- we'll eat turkey?" I yawned and looked around. Several people were getting out of the plane.
"Oh gosh! The luggage would be arriving now! All those clothes and stuff!" she cried and shook me.

"Hmm…" I muttered and stretched widely.

"Darling, get your rucksack- yes there it is - and follow dad off the plane. I need to find my phone and text Granny and Grandad."

She said, busily fumbling inside her bag. I silently followed my dad out of the plane and a group of hushed rumours followed me.

India was a great place, nice and sunny, and I missed my grandparents. I hoped that they would come soon. Mosquitoes zoomed in and out of my eyesight and the blinding sun was warming me up. I felt very hot and poured a bit of water on top of my head. I instantly felt better. I dragged my suitcase over to Lucy and she helpfully put it onto a trolley. We collected our things and rushed off to the exit.

Lucy begged for a doughnut from the nearby store and she put heaps of sauce and sprinkles on top. I took a small cookie and nibbled the edge, uncertainly staring at the sky. My mum was doing the same.

"Er- Jadie, Julie? What are you looking at?" my dad asked nervously, as many other people tried to follow our gaze. I shook myself.

"Nothing… nothing at all- just that it is very… bright!" I lied and nudged my mum.

"Yes. Veeeery bright. Yes." She nodded distractedly.

"OK." My dad did not look completely sure. He and Lucy swapped bewildered looks that clearly read: *These people have gone loopy.*

I didn't mind. I went along. Avoiding everyone's gazes and finally spotted my grandparents.

"Grandma! Grandpa" I shouted joyfully. I bounded towards them and into their embrace. My grandfather is a robust, stockily built man who is good with Engineering and can always make things better. He is 73 years old. His name is Sunil.

My grandma is a jolly, merry person who was deeply into reading. She was wearing a glimmering, neon saree and her half-moon, gold spectacles. She beamed at me over them. Her name is Sabrina, and she is 67 years old.

"Jadie! You're so big!" she told me and embraced me. My grandpa did the same. Then, they did the same to Lucy and began talking rapidly to my parents. They are my mum's parents and grandma speaks in a machine-gun, rapid sort of way. My dad looked like she was talking gibberish. He looked politely confused.

We went into their car and drove past lots of towns and villages. The road was filled with cars, taxis, and *several* animals. The first thing I saw was a horse, dragging a cart full of sugarcanes behind him. The man on the cart was yelling and urging the horse to go faster. He spoke in Hindi, and I only understood a few words he said. I saw some lonely cows nearby, eating from the palm of a little girl standing next to them. I smiled. It seemed perfect. People in sarees and people in colourful clothes bustled about.

"Geez, it's quite chilly here, isn't it?" my dad asked, shivering slightly. I stared at him. India was literally known for its hot weather.

"It is boiling! Take off the mittens dad, nobody else is wearing them!" I replied, trying to force off his mitts.

"Nope." He grinned and went to talk to Lucy. My grandparents were waving brightly to everyone and were smiling happily. My mum's worried look melted off her face, but mine didn't exactly. My eyes were still searching the sky.

I shrugged and looked around. We arrived at my grandparent's mansion and a maid welcomed us in.

My grandpa's brother lives in the next house. I breathed in the familiar scents of fabulous cooking, sweet flowers and freshly cut grass. I ran to my mum's old bedroom and fell onto the snug, soft bed contentedly. Outside, crows squawked, asking my grandma for some rice. She feeds them every day before her morning walk.

My grandma went to make some delicious, juicy sweets and was singing merrily. My dad came in the room to put some suitcases beneath the bed. I idly looked out of the window and saw a tuft of gleaming, familiar black hair whizz out of sight. I gripped the suitcase I was holding and sat on the bed hurriedly. I saw the owner of the black hair grin into the window.

It was Mira.

13. Mira

I gasped at the window before darting out of the room. My grandma called me to taste some of her tasty sweets. My tummy rumbled but I ignored it.

"MIRA!" I shouted joyfully and I sprang towards her. She looked around and joy flashed across her face. She ran over to me, and I stooped down, allowing her to climb onto my hand.

"Where-how-why-what?" I stammered as she looked up at me in amazement.
"Well, it was all part of our parents' plan. I thought you knew. We come to this part of the world every year to see my grandparents and uncles and aunts. This time, we found a friend, close to where you were heading. I thought your parents would have told you." Mira told me. I felt a bit sad for being kept in the dark. My grandma rushed out of the house and saw me and Mira.
"My, my…. Is this your friend? I do feel like I know her too!" she said and came down the steps, carefully avoiding her handmade rangoli pattern on the floor. "She looks like my friend Priya!"

I was glad that my grandma could only see Mira as a normal sized 11-year-old.
"Are you Mira Partail?" she asked.
"Um yes. And Priya is my grandma." Mira replied uncertainly, looking sideways at me.
"Oh, hello Mira! I have heard everything about you from my daughter and granddaughter…" my grandma said brightly, shaking Mira's hand excitedly. Mira grinned awkwardly.

"Why don't you two go and tell her mum and dad to join us for lunch. Oh, and give them these!" Grandma offered two fantastic sweets and hurried off. We stood in silence.

"Well... your grandma seems very cheerful." Mira suggested. I nodded. "let's go and deliver these sweets."

I was introduced to Mira's family friend. Her name was Rupa.

"Thank you so much for inviting us, dear! Your granny is Sabrina, right? I know her! She was my old colleague before we went into retirement! You can come in while I change and get ready for lunch! Yes sure, I'll come, thank you! Mira's mum and dad are busy unpacking and getting things organised, but I'll be happy to come along." beamed Rupa. She was a smiley, cheerful lady who was wearing way too much make up. I was sure my grandma wouldn't mind that Rupa was joining us for lunch instead of the parents.

We hurried inside and sat on Mira's bed. I was still trembling in shock.

"So, explain everything," we said in unison.
"No, you go first." Mira said.
"No, you." I retorted.
She sighed, "What is there to explain? Every summer, I go to India to visit my family. I don't know exactly how long we're staying here but it is definitely not permanent. This time, it had to be Rupa and Rohan, as our mums had planned that we stay close. My grandparents must be wondering why we haven't visited them yet. I told you back at the hotel that you would be seeing me sooner than you expected. I thought you knew," She winked.

"Fine. But, what about the gem?" I asked, something like panic and excitement creeping into my throat.

"Oh, that," Mira's face fell. She gripped my arm tightly, "Jadie. It's gone."

14. Hawk!

"What do you mean?" I asked, my heart dropping.

"Like I said, it's gone. I looked in exactly where you said, and it wasn't there. I bet you anything that one of *them* did it." She glowered at me.

I was thinking hard when Rupa came in. I fell silent but Mira seemed perfectly at ease even though Rupa came in while we were in the middle of such a deep conversation.

"Your Mumsy is coming to say hello to Jadie!" she beamed at us. Mira rolled her eyes and gritted her teeth. Her mum appeared, literally 2 seconds after.
"Oh, Hi Jadie! How are you? Where is your mum?" she asked beaming at me.
"I'm ok. Mum is at home… I mean, grandma's home. But I think she was about to set out for some shopping and seeing some old friends. That's what she usually does on holiday." I said and gave a false grin.

She gave a rather curious look at me and then shrugged inwardly. I felt rather overwrought. She stared at me for one more moment before slinging a posh shoulder bag over her arm. She smiled.

"I heard your grandma kindly invited us. Let's go. I'll come too," she said. And so, we all went.

"Rupa! What a surprise!" My grandmother beamed as we all sat down at the table. Lunch was served. It was simply delectable. I shovelled down an abundant amount of food and saw that Mira was doing the same.

"Finished." We said in unison. We glared at each other.

"Um… no pudding?" my grandpa asked, rather crestfallen. I couldn't bear that look.

"Um, why not." I said and sat down, ignoring Mira's cold eyes. As soon as I finished, we ran off and sat in the garden, up a tree.

"Odd position, but if you insist." She had said and settled down.

"So, the gem wasn't there." I said, in a matter-of-fact way.

"Yes." She sighed, "How many times?"

"So, do you think that there is a possibility that Jake or Liam took it?" I asked.

"You idiot Jadie. I shall pretend that I didn't hear you," She snapped, "of course, they didn't take it, they would tell us."

"Anyway…" she continued briskly, "Woah, this is kind of sounding like me and you solving a mystery from one of those books, right?" I shook my head.

"Well, I need to tell you something, Jadie. Don't get mad at me. I need to go back to England! And I need to go as soon as possible. Don't give me that look and don't ask me any questions!" she growled and furiously ran her hands in her hair.

"That is impossible Mira." I retorted

"Humph. For you maybe. But I survived a curse for a week." She complained. "If anyone can achieve anything, it is me. Not you. You just give up. The adults think they can help me, but I really doubt anyone can. Yes, I know I told your mum everything, but no one can help now."

Fuming, I slid down the branch and landed on the floor with a thump. I had no idea how Mira was going to get down. But I didn't care. I knew that there was no way that Mira could possibly fly back to England in less than a day. Unless... no Mira wouldn't do that.

She's a good girl. She wouldn't do anything that crazy... She wouldn't fly- no that was a silly idea.

Just then I heard a familiar voice. "Hello Jadie. Where is Mira?" her mum asked icily.

"She went to the- loo." I said and tried to look neutral.

"Well... tell her to come home when she is finished. Daisy needs feeding and I need to go. She can stay for five extra minutes if she wants to but no more." She said briskly. I knew all about Daisy. Mira had told me that she was Rupa's dog and that Mira adored her.

I nodded and went out into the garden.

"Um... Jadie? Can you get me down?" a tiny voice spoke out.

I grimaced and got a box from inside. I got Mira down and put her in the box.

"What?" she asked, her voiced muffled.

I didn't reply. I raced just outside Mira's street. I dropped the box, opened the lid, and ran back. It was only about 200 metres, but the air was arid, which gave me an urge to drink 10 bottles of cool water. When I got back, my grandmother was waiting, with her vigilant eyes.

"Where have you been?" she asked.

"I walked Mira back." I gasped.

"Is the girl incapable of walking herself about a quarter of a kilometre?" She asked testily. I didn't reply but hurried under her arm into the open door.

The television was on and blaring brightly. It was the news.

"-appearance of a team of hawks flying around India. There is a beautiful one in the middle who seems to be the leader and the ornithologists have informed us that it is a short-tailed- species and is one of the rarest ever. They are landing in Bangalore tonight so keep your eyes peeled. Mary Jean Smith, the manager of the 'Ornithology team' has informed us that no one can claim this hawk as it has already got an owner, Mrs Charlotte Grace. She had lost her pet and would like it back immediately. She will speak to us about this rare and beautiful bird. If you want to know more about this rare bird, please wait as we bring you someone from all the way in England who knows more."

My mum and me stared at each other in silence.

He passed the microphone to the lady standing next to him. She had heaps of make up on. She looked just like Nephia but had literally doused herself with mascara and eyeshadow. Her eyes glittered. She was wearing a red handbag filled with bottles and was looking at the camera with a smirk.

"Well, I live in England with my hawk …Tim. He is a rare species, and he is tamed by using this piece of honey. I normally must make plenty of honey for him. He'll do anything to get it! We've both

lived most of our lives at our Hotel Srakolian. He is so dear to me, and I have been tearing my hair out to find him! I have seen him on the news, and I am desperately trying to reach out to him. I can't believe that my darling bird has been able to fly to India! I see him in the sky sometimes as I have travelled to India and tried to coax him down… but no luck! Such a shame. I must say a little thank you to everyone who has helped me. Best wishes to all from my wonderful Hotel Srakolian and…"

The television was switched off. Everyone looked at my mum.

"That's not her hotel, its mum's!" I yelled, rising to my feet, and glowering at everyone unexpectedly.

"MUM DIDN'T GIVE IT TO ANYONE! EVERYONE KNOWS! TELL 'EM MUM! TELL THEM DAD. I DON'T- WE'VE NEVER HAD STUPID CHARLOTTE GRACE IN THE HOTEL!" I bellowed. Everyone gasped. I ran away, sobbing quietly and buried myself under the masses of blanket that covered me from sight and gave me comfort. I was upset and tired and must have fallen asleep. Jet lag maybe.

I woke up with a start. Bright waves of gold flooded through the glass. I yawned. I remembered what had happened and scowled. I dressed and traipsed down to the kitchen. Only my mum was at the table. She nodded at me. She seemed very lost in thought. I felt suddenly ashamed of my little tantrum last night. I winced. She seemed to be in strange mood. I sighed. I sat down, ate my porridge, and went outside.

I decided to visit Mira after our little argument yesterday.

Mr Partail opened the door.

"Um… Hi!" I said in a queer voice that was unlike my own. "May I see Mira?"

"She has gone out for a bit and says that she doesn't want to be disturbed." Mr Partail said to me smiling in a rather strained way, "She is a bit upset."

My stomach dropped. "Well, I… um…wanted to give a… marble which she forgotten at my grandparent's house." I lied.

He frowned.

"Well, Mira does like collecting marbles. All right, you know that park near your house? Well, go through the alleyway and she should be sitting on a bench reading. That is what she said she would be doing." He said, "Give her that marble."

"Oooh." I shivered as I went into the alleyway.

I had to unwillingly show Mira's dad my own special marble for proof. I knew that Mira collected marbles from the time she could probably pick stuff up. Same as me.

"Mira!" I gasped skidding to a halt. I gaped. There was an empty bench and no one on it. A book lay on the bench, forgotten.

Then, I heard someone familiar cough from behind.
"Mira!" I cried.
There she was, as small as a grass blade.
"Oh, hi Jadie." She said in a constricted voice.

There was an awkward silence.

"Look, I am sorry about yesterday. Honestly. I shouldn't have yelled back. I should have tried to listen and understand." I said apologetically and trying to make eye contact with her.

"No, it is fine." Mira replied stiffly turning herself slightly away from me.

I stared. That was something Mira would never have said. She was acting strange.

"Look Jadie, as I said yesterday, I need to get to England. Fast. You said that it was impossible. It is not. I have found a way." She began steadily.

My heart plummeted, "So… am I going to come too? Can you tell me what it is?" I asked sceptically.

"Well…" she seemed to be choosing her words carefully. And slowly.

This annoyed me.

"Oh, come on, just spit it out! You're being a brat now! Just tell me now Mira! Where's Liam? Where's Jake? What is wrong with you? You're-" I never managed to finish my sentence.

She had quelled me with a sharp, penetrating stare which she had never done before.

"Mira?" I asked cautiously.
"Follow me. I shall show you how I will travel back. Come now." She said in icy tones. Her jaw was clenched, and she had turned rather pale. Without bothering to check if I was following, she marched swiftly across the grass. I struggled to keep up, even though she was about 10 times smaller than me.

After a good 10 minutes, she stopped and pointed at a tree. It was thick and there was a matted swamp of brambles in about the middle. The blazing sun hindered me in looking up.

I looked at Mira. She looked calm and the sun's light shone on her face as the wind brushed her tresses backwards. I was baffled. She looked at me, her face fathomless.

"Look up." She commanded. I, ignoring the sun's glares did so.
And almost fell over. Circling the tree was none other than Hawk Everdark.
"Mira! Get away from him now!" I gasped.

"No." her face was tranquil and showed no expression. The hawk circled the tree one more time and flew down onto her shoulder. She looked at it sharply. Then, in a flash, Hawk Everdark stood beside her, wearing a dark cloak, and was smiling eerily at me.

"Why, good morning, Miss Hills. I was just having a little chat with young Miss Partail about how she was going to get back to England." He smiled.
"Whaaaa…." I croaked.
"I will fly Miss Mira back to England in about 5 minutes. Don't worry, I swear I will not hurt her."
"And you won't hurt Jadie, Jake and Liam." Mira added.
"Yes, of course. Now when are we leaving?" he asked coldly.
Waves of relief washed over me. At least she still didn't want me harmed. Or the boys of course. But I couldn't trust Hawk entirely. I didn't want us to be separated again.

"No, Mira. Please!" I pleaded.

"Jadie. It is ok. I just need that gem. I want to be myself... my proper size. I don't want to keep hiding my size from people. You're still my friend. I have not turned evil. I swear. Don't follow. I'll be fine. I just don't think any of you can help me." She muttered, her eyes averting mine but shining with tears.

"I will be back soon... as myself." She gave me a hug and turned to Hawk.

"Let's go."

She turned to me, her face steady and full of determination. Her eyes locked with mine for the last time. She turned to Hawk but now he was a giant bird, waiting and watching silently.

She clambered onto the Hawk and looked over at India.

"Goodbye dear friend."
And with that, the great bird turned around soared into the sky with Mira clinging on.

"Noooooooo! Mira!"

I shouted, tears rolling down my face and my heart heavy with grief and anger. I watched helplessly as the two flew out of my sight.

15. An encounter in my bedroom

I don't know how long I stayed there, but at some point, heavy rain pounded the ground and me. I lay on the ground, hoping bitterly for it to swallow me up. My hair was plastered to my face and rainwater mixed with the tears. I sniffled, calling her name repeatedly and yelled into the sky.

After hours, I heaved myself up and tried to walk home, with jelly-like legs and the mud pulling at my shoes. I didn't care that my clothes were ruined or what my mum would say. I just walked and walked.

"JADIE!" my mum shrieked as she opened the front door. "You're soaked! Drenched to the bone! You're all muddy and filthy! What happened? It's almost dinner!"

I just clambered into the house and looked dully at her.
"Is it Mira?" What happened? Jadie-"
"OOOOHHH! WHERE'S LITTLE JADIE! IS SHE HURT? IS SHE OK? WHERE'S LITTLE BABY JADIE WADIE?" my grandmother screamed, running into the porch, and squashing me into an enormous bear hug.
"You're wet! Soaking! Were you outside? We've been looking for you everywhere!" she squealed, "Paul? PAUL! GET A TOWEL!" she screeched, "It is Jadie! Quickly!"

My dad came dashing into the porch, with a grey, scruffy towel in his hands. He hastily draped it around me and began speaking in rapid Hindi to my mum.

"Jadie! Tell us what happened! Get dry and come and have some food!" my grandmother said urgently. My grandfather came pelting into the room, his arms laden in sweets and food. He gasped at the sight of me and ran over.

"Jadie! Tell us what happened! Get dry and come and have some food!" he said.

"No. I'm fine. I'll just get dry. I'm okay." I moaned and tried to push past them. "I just got caught in the rain when I went to the park."

My grandfather pushed an armful of clothes into my hands. It took me a moment to realise that it was my pyjamas.

They were dark blue and deep red, patterned with wave-like swirls. I grimaced and went to put them on. When I came back, they ushered me inside and threw a heavy, silky blanket over my shoulders.

"Come sit on the couch." My dad said gently.

I lay down and shivered uncontrollably. I started to perspire and tried to push the blanket off me. It had hues of gold streaked across the red velvet. I shoved it off and got up... and fell over immediately. My mum grabbed me quickly.

"Sit down." She said caringly.
"No." I murmured into her ear. "Please. I need to tell you something."
She excused us saying she needed to dry my hair and quickly dragged me off to her room.
"Right, what is it?" she asked facing me with a worried look.
"It is Mira, mum. She went with Hawk Everdark. Back to England so that she could get the gem and fix her size. He promised not to harm her, but I don't believe it. She is taking his help as she doesn't think we can help. But then,

she may join their side. She is going to turn dark, mum! *Evil*. I need to see her and try and stop her!"

My mum was silent for a while. "Well, if she is taking a lift…"

"Why don't you take a lift too? I won't harm you! Just like Hawk won't harm your friend Mira. Come on little one. Come here." A voice cooed in the shadows.

Then, out stepped Nephia Everdark.

"Hi darling! And you Julie! Lovely to see you both." she said brightly, pulling off a deep magenta cloak off her squared shoulders. I could only stare in horror. My mum, however, threw her arms in front of me and snarled, "Get away from her, you horrible, evil-"

"I came here by shadow travel." She interrupted, disregarding my mum's thunderstorm-like expression.
"Now Julie, Jadie. J's. The two J's. Don't be frightened. I won't hurt you here. Promise. Plus, I am only here to help." She pouted and smiled pleasantly. "Your friend Mira got a lift, what about you?"
"No thanks." I said coldly. "Please go."
I didn't expect her to.
"Not leaving dear, but maybe if you come. Please?" she asked, her eyes widening in a trying-to-be-cute manner.
"Why do you want me?" I asked shrewdly.
"I want to help." She said after a second. My mum gave a sarcastic cough.
"The *real* reason please?" asked my mum.

Nephia narrowed her eyes and her mouth twitched. I watched as her hand drifted to her red handbag.

"Fine. I need you." She said coldly, all the sweetness evaporating.

"Why? For what?" I asked, hoping my eyes were narrowing menacingly.

"For two reasons. Firstly, I need you to come for this little… event, which does *not* involve you or any of your friends and family getting hurt. This… event will enable me to make the final potion that will make me the magical world's most talented potion maker. But don't worry. I will only use the potion after your time, in a different world. Far away from Earth. I swear. Secondly, I cannot take the gem out. I need you to take it out for me. But don't worry, it will only be after Mira has taken the gem and used it. I won't hurt you or your friends and family. Of course, that's only if you help me." She told me calmly.

"What do you mean 'after my time'?" I asked.

"When you live your long life and die *naturally*." She said flatly. There was silence that followed those words.

"So where do you come from?" my mum asked sceptically.

"From a planet far from Earth, in a different galaxy. My potion will anyway only work there." she replied.

"How will I help you take the gem? Why can't you take it out?" I asked, rather curiously.

"Because Samra's blood runs through you. You are the only living soul who can fetch the gem out of the pillar. Plus, I need a teeny tiny drop of your blood to make that ultimate potion!!!! It won't hurt and… you don't really have a choice." She answered impatiently, as though I was supposed to accept all this.

"Wait! Does that mean that you'll take out my blood or something?" I asked, terror creeping into my voice.

"You're not hurting her. You won't!" My mum said, stepping in front of me.

"Stand aside you silly girl!" shouted Nephia warningly.

"NO!" my mum said, taking a little step backwards.

But Nephia was too quick. She whipped out a bottle and threw it with all her might. It landed at my mum's feet and seeped into her velvet slippers. A moment later, my mum had flown on the bed and was snoring loudly. Nephia took a step towards me.

"Come," She said, "Before I do worse. If you do come with me right now, your mum will be absolutely fine." She added.

I closed my eyes and screwed up my face. I didn't want anyone else to get hurt. She had promised not to hurt me or anyone else. She promised that my mum would wake up and be perfectly fine. I felt that everything was already horribly wrong, but it could get worse if I didn't obey. I was trapped. I looked at Nephia intently. Slowly. I nodded.

"Good child," She whispered. "Mira's already there."

16. Death

The travel was about thirty seconds, but every moment seemed like a day. At last, we reached. I wriggled out of Nephia's icy grasp and ran towards my previous home. All that was left of the prodigious Museum was a heap of ash strewn on the floor. I sniffed. This made everything real. I looked up at the building and saw that new words now replaced '**Hotel Saturn**'. It now read in flashing letters:

Institution for the needy.

Inside was a myriad of people looking out of the window, placing their belongings in rooms and all sorts. I saw something rather odd. The room that I used to stay in was empty and the lights were off. So was my mum's study. And the window where Nephia had stayed had vanished.

"Come on!" Nephia growled and dragged me over to the shed, that had remained intact. "Hurry up! Hawk's waiting!"

I walked over to the shed and stepped inside. And gaped. The shed, where we had once shovelled heaps of dirt into, was huge on the inside. It was immaculate and perfect. I gasped at the makeover: 2 spectacular double beds, an unblemished ensuite, a living room and a kitchen. The whole area was about the size of a football pitch. Behind the beds was the stone pillar. It was *the pillar*. Looking perfect.

There were two sofas. Hawk Everdark sat on one and opposite him sat Mira, her eyes fixed on the stone. (at least she didn't look like she had made friends with Hawk). I sat down next to Mira, and she slipped her hand into mine. Nephia sat next to Hawk and stared at us beadily.

"Right kids. We give Mira back her true size – she gets the gem from the pillar, uses it, and restores herself. Then you give us back the gem and get out of here. And you will never see us again. Deal?" she asked.

I hesitated. I opened my mouth. What was the deal? What else did they want from us? Or me? Mira was nodding and I couldn't say anything. I wanted her to be herself again.

"No." A boy with shaggy, sun-bleached hair and football shorts crossed the room. I gasped. The boy looked at me with familiar, blue eyes. Then, a second boy came over, shaking chestnut brown hair out of his eyes. He looked scathingly at the terrible two.
"No. It's wrong. Not right. You're just evil and foul." Liam West said to Nephia, crossing his arms and glaring at her.
"Yeah, you can't do that. You're a power-hungry monster." Jake White added.
"Guilty." Whispered Nephia softly leaning forward. I shuddered. Then, Hawk Everdark stood up and jerked his fingers upwards. A metal cage plummeted downwards and enveloped the four of us.
"Now children. I don't want to hear anymore from the silly boys. Don't test what I can do when I'm angry." Nephia said from below. She raised her arms and the cage tilted. I fell out and landed on the carpet. Except that it just felt like landing on a giant, squishy pancake.

"As we have reached an agreement, Jadie Hills, I would like us to drink together." She said, pretending to sound warm. A glass of water landed on their coffee table as she spoke. I lifted it up with trembling fingers. As I lifted it, Mira fell out of the cage.

Without a moment's hesitation, she grabbed me and ran towards the stone pillar. Neither Everdarks stopped us. She reached the great stone and reached towards the gem. It bypassed her and flew to my hands, flickering red, yellow, blue, and purple. I knew why it had gone around her. I felt truly thrilled and almost powerful! It was because I was Samra's descendant. I had magic running through my bones. I was the great granddaughter of someone magical and I was the only living soul who could get the gem out of the pillar. So, ignoring her crestfallen, disbelieving face, I struggled to hide my glee and triumph. I gave it to her and then, her whole body began to glow with silver light. She was bathed in a glimmering aura. Then, the gem seemed to peel away from its former self and transformed into a diamond. Nephia gave a snort in a mocking but impressed way.

"Only a truly worthy person can do that. She'll be back to normal." She said in her icy cold way.
"What do you mean?" I asked.
"Well, it's supposed to stop the curse. Now she's gonna be back to her true size. For everyone to see her in the same way. Easy!"

I smiled happily. Mira grinned at me, a true smile. Then, her body began to grow, back to her former self.
"Wow! Wizard!" she yelled and bounded over to me. She gave me a hug.
"Now, drink the glass Jadie." Nephia said firmly. I had forgotten about it.
"You swear that you're not giving me poison?

"I swear." Nephia replied casually. I wondered if she was telling the truth and hoped she was. I looked into her eyes and saw truthfulness inside them. But as the glass was near my lips, I thought I saw a glimmer of something else in them. Something that didn't seem right.

But it was too late. When I was about to put the glass down, Hawk Everdark bounded forwards and shoved the glass to my lips. It didn't hurt at all when he did it but the moment my lips touched the glass, it evaporated, and I suddenly got a happy feeling and felt tranquil and calm. My vision began to dim and blur but I didn't mind. I couldn't think properly and just wanted sleep. I slowly closed my eyes. I heard someone yelling. Was it Mira? Or just my own mind telling me to go sleep? I didn't want to give it too much thought. I was too sleepy. I gave a huge yawn, and everything went black.

17. The final battle

"Is she dead? Is she going to wake up? Did it work?" I heard a voice say in anguish. I could hear someone sobbing in the background. "Do you think that it didn't work?" the voice repeated. I groggily opened my eyes and looked around, rubbing sleep from my eyes.

"J A D I E !!!!!!!!" a voice shrieked, and I felt something barrel into me. If I didn't recognise the voice, I would have said an elephant barged into me. The sheer joy of Mira was enough to send me rolling about on the sofa, that I was lying on.

"What happened?" I muttered.
"Well… um sorry to say that you… er… passed away." Jake said apologetically.
"Mira was in floods." Liam added.
"I was not!" she scowled as she furiously wiped rivers of tears off her cheeks while trying to hide them.
"What do you mean?" I asked.
"You died." Liam said patting me on the shoulder.
"WHAT?" I shouted, giving them incredulous stare, "I only closed my eyes for like… 5 seconds."

"No! It wasn't 5 seconds. Oh my gosh, what an intense and crazy time we had!" Liam was shouting with excitement.
"So, why am I alive?" I asked, frowning slightly.
"Because I am the smartest person in the world." Jake coolly said, pretending to straighten an imaginary tie.
"No, you are not! It was all my idea." complained Mira.
"Fair enough." Jake sighed and grinned toothily at Mira.

"Well, anyway, I threatened to break the gem and-" Mira began.

"Yikes!" I shouted. I had just noticed something etched into my skin.

"What?" Mira, Jake, and Liam asked.

I indicated an almost healed gash on my arm. It looked as though the skin had been cut and hastily healed.

"Oh, I was getting to that," Mira said, "So they gave me a resurrection potion. But on the way... Hawk dropped a dagger into your arm. He gave a so-called yelp of surprise to act like it was an accident and picked the dagger out. He then dropped a bit of... um... blood into Nephia's bottle and they vanished, leaving the resurrection potion behind them." Mira said.

"Wait a minute," I said, memories flooding back, "Let's start at the very beginning. Nephia promised that it wasn't poison. But was the drink poisonous?"

"Um... I don't think it was..." Jake said uncertainly.
"So, wait. They got me to fetch the stone, then they somehow kind of knocked me out, then attacked me to get a drop of my blood and left me to die?" I asked in shock and horror.
"Well no... not really. They did all that to you, stole the stone from Mira but left us with a resurrection potion. I think that's because Mira threatened to smash the gem and there was no way they could grab it from her. They really wanted it. So, they swapped the gem for the resurrection potion." said Jake. The others were agreeing and nodding.

I looked at Mira with gratitude as she traded the gem for my life. She knew I was feeling thankful.

"How long ago did they leave?" I asked nervously.

"About 5 hours ago." Mira sniffed miserably.

"WHAT?" I shouted.

"Nah… don't be ridiculous Mira. I am the one with a watch here. Jadie's been dead for about one hour." Jake said breezily, squeezing her shoulders.

"OW! I'm sorry! I don't have a watch on!" Mira snapped, batting his hands away in frustration.

"Wait! What's that?" I said suddenly, pointing to the wall.

"That was where they vanished.' Mira said.

"No! There is a bit of black smoke!" I yelled.

"Woah! She's right Mira!" Jake yelled in surprise.

"Fancy that! We've been here for *apparently* 5 hours and Jadie just got resurrected. And she spotted it first! Our eyesight must be terrible and-"

He stopped as Mira gave him a kick and shot him a murderous stare that read: SHUT UP, don't overdo it.

I think they were trying to make me feel better.

I thought hard about how they must have vanished, leaving behind a trace of black smoke. I just hoped for dear life that because of my magical heritage, I would have the ability to magically travel wherever I wanted to, in the depths of darkness. If Nephia could, I could.

"Come on guys! All we must do is to get inside that last bit of smoke and concentrate on… just concentrate." I commanded.

"On what? Where are we going in a puff of smoke?" Mira asked sardonically.

"Guys, we need to finish this. We have come this far, and we have each other. Come on, please. Let's find them and destroy them forever," I pleaded, "set your mind on Nephia." I said firmly.

We all stepped into the fumes, and I fixed my mind on Nephia (it was not a pretty sight.) Then, I felt my body move and suddenly, I could only see darkness. I could no longer feel 3 hands clutching mine. Then… I tumbled out of the smoke. Blinking and coughing, I saw it move away, with 1… 2 people inside. Oh no, did we all not make it?

"Woah… what is this place?" a voice asked, tugging at my sleeve. I jumped and saw Liam.

"I dunno. Hey! Where's Jake and Mira?' I asked, focusing on the place where the dark smoke had been, but it had gone, "Hey Liam! Where *are* they?" I wondered if Nephia had done some sort of potion on it. I immediately started worrying.

"Meh… they'll find us in the end." Liam said, looking unconcerned. I looked around and immediately recognised it as one of the streets near my grandparents' house. I could see the hospital towering above us. I didn't expect to land here. I didn't expect Nephia to have chosen to be here.

"Did you think of Nephia?" I asked Liam.

"No. I thought of home. Sorry Jadie, I tried to think of Nephia, but I couldn't," Liam replied, "Mum making delicious puddings and me eating heaps of caramel and sticky, toffee cake and… yeah."

"It's okay Liam. I thought of Nephia, and I think my thoughts have brought us to her. Sadly, it wasn't enough to bring the other two." I replied. Poor Liam.

I looked around and saw that we were in a busy city. There was a shop and it read:

Danielle's DELECTABLE DELIGHTS.

I wondered if Liam's thoughts had brought us to this cake shop. We walked inside. There was a downstairs area where you could order your food and an upstairs seating. As I expected, there was only one table that was occupied. 2 people sat there, drinking tea from a chipped cup. The lady had her eyes covered by an expensive cap. She lifted it off her head slightly and looked me in the eye. Hers turned crimson.

"Why are you staring at that couple?" Liam asked, nudging me painfully in the ribs.

"Cause they're not a couple." I whispered back. He got the message.

"Great." He gulped. He kept on shooting looks at the two though. We bought a small cookie each and settled at the table furthest away from Nephia and Hawk. None of them looked surprised to see us. I expected a bit more recognition. *I had just died and come alive!* Then, as soon as we finished our cookies, the two people (if you could call them people) got up and left down the stairs.

"Now what?" Liam asked.

"Duh. We follow them." I said, trying to sound confident. I was positively petrified but I tried not to show it. The lightbulb, that dangled in the air above us suddenly switched off and we were plunged into utter darkness. I fumbled for Liam's hands as we made our way down the stairs. I fell down the last 3 but luckily fell on something else. Or should I say, 'somebody else?'

"Get off me you great lump." Liam moaned he shook me off.

"Oops." I said trying not to laugh. The lights turned on. We stood up, blinking in the light and saw Nephia and Hawk, staring hungrily at us. The café owners were nowhere to be seen. I noticed the light in the room was too bright, so I looked up. Above us, a cage was suspended, made from what looked like wooden sticks. I saw with shock and horror that Mira and Jake were inside; Mira was radiating light from all directions and her face was ghostly and pale. She didn't move and her eyes were glassy and unfocused. I felt a small pang of relief that they were at least around us.

"What happened?" I asked, looking at them and cowering against the wall. Liam did the same.

"Well darling... You see, we backtracked on our words slightly. Mira annoyed us by threatening to smash the coveted gem. So, once we got the gem off her, my dearest granddaughter used a special potion that would take Mira back to the 'cursed state.' But... so far... it has just given her a sort of ghostly appearance. She'll be teeny tiny soon. Oh, and I thought she needed a friend in there." Hawk said.

"So now we have your blood and the gem, we can get back to our beautiful planet. But we are having so much fun here, so we decided to hang around for a bit and see if we could get rid of all of you. Once and for all... We can then pursue our exploits elsewhere!" Her words hung in the air.

"WHAT?" I shouted, "Why are you so evil? Why do you hate us so much? Why don't you leave us and go away?"

She paused. A dreamy look came over her face and her eyes became unfocused.

"Why? I don't know Jadie Hills. That's a good question... Perhaps it's because you're related to SAMRA, and we HATE him!" she yelled suddenly.

She lurched forwards, knocking me off my feet. It caught my surprise, I fell, and banged my head against the wall. Yellow stars popped in front of my eyes and my head span. I heard Liam gasp, and I felt a throbbing pain on my head. Gasping in pain, I watched helplessly as Nephia pinned me against the wall as Hawk walked menacingly towards us. His black, fathomless eyes bore into my own.

She grabbed my throat and held her head close to mine. "Well, Jadie Hills... not as strong and powerful as I thought you were. You're just weak... pathetic and blinded by friendship." She whispered, her face inches from mine.

"You'll never w-win! We-We'll- s-stop y-you!" I choked, hardly able to breathe, let alone speak.

"Maybe, if you live a moment longer..." Nephia said, her red eyes gleaming. Her angular cheekbones were slowly turning paler and paler. Her cascade of midnight tresses blew around her face and she gave a snarl.

"You promised not to hurt me!" I croaked.
"And we haven't, at least before you died. Now, the oath has died along with you." Hawk smirked. He gave a little shake of his head, throwing hair out of his eyes and locked eyes with me. I didn't know where to look. Into those cold eyes of death? Or my friends' pale, half-dead bodies. Neither gave me relief. Then, just as my eyes

travelled to Hawk's pocket, I heard a small hissing noise, as if there was some steam that was coming out a pressure cooker. Though, it was a lot quieter. It was then when I saw a forked tongue lash out at my ankles. I looked down properly and saw a horrible, vast rattlesnake curling slowly around my ankles. I uttered a silent scream and tried not to look down. Nephia gave a cruel grin.

I exhaled slowly. Liam, who had been standing watching, had now turned deathly pale and his teeth were chattering. Mira still looked unfocused and lost.

She had now turned green, and her hair was floating around her, her face now in mid-scream. I shivered. Jake was next to her and was fortunately moving one of his eyeballs around. He kept on staring at me, then Mira then… who knows what. I didn't know what to do. Keep talking and play for time, give up, try to run or… wait until I had more options. I decided to wait. Nephia stared at me, her eyes running down my body and examining, waiting to pounce. Hawk sat on a chair and gave an eery smile at Liam. Poor Liam's eyes widened and he presently fainted, falling with a thud on the cold, hard floor. The snake gradually disentangled itself from me and slipped towards Liam, who was practically translucent. It coiled beside him but did not go near him thankfully. It looked at me as if saying: *If you make one wrong move, he is dead.*

Nephia gave a malicious laugh, which made me jump. I had literally been hypnotised by the snake's movements, "All alone Jadie… Mummy's knocked out, Jake's captured, Liam's fainted and Mira's more dead than alive…"

Suddenly anger surged into my limbs. I felt angrier and more intense than ever. My fear was drowned in a wave of passion and wrath. Nephia's laugh faltered as my eyes shone with fury. "DON'T YOU DARE SPEAK ABOUT THEM IN FRONT OF ME!" I roared.

Without a moment's hesitation, I leapt at Nephia, pinning her against the wall. My mind burned and my head spun. I could vaguely hear Hawk yelling, but I didn't pay attention. Then, an ancient, wise voice whispered:
FIGHT FOR THE RIGHT

Next, I felt my head spin and I felt weightless and dizzy. Then, my head began to clear-quickly. My vision began to sharpen, sharper than before and I felt like a pack of cards, first being shuffled, shuffled so much that you begin to feel disconnected and empty… then, as it arranges itself and you feel perfectly orientated. Suddenly, I felt a strange feeling, bubbling up my chest like a volcano. It felt warm and tangy, sweet, and beautiful. It made me feel wonderful and loved. I looked at Nephia in the eye for one last time. She looked back, her eyes as cold as steel. The warm, passionate feeling had reached its peak, growing immeasurably in my chest. As Nephia's eyes locked with mine, I thought of Samra… and charged. Before I had even finished my first step, I felt my vision blur and dim. It didn't feel like dying… just like letting someone else think for my body. Just before everything went completely dark, I saw Nephia, staring in horror at something, her expression full of terror. Hawk suddenly saw whatever she was seeing and uttered a silent scream. It probably was deafening, but I couldn't hear him. Then, it all went black.

My eyes opened and I was standing up, bent over two bodies. They belonged to Nephia and Hawk. They were both fading, evaporating in seconds. I gave a weak grin and aimed a kick at Nephia (who was the closest). My foot never touched her. Instead, it passed through thin air. Then, I heard someone cough behind me. Mira and Jake had fallen to the floor, Liam was standing up. But it wasn't just the three of them; there were four people.

"Well done Jadie Hills. You've made us proud. Mira, Jake, and Liam are perfectly fine. So is my dear Julie. I'm happy to tell you that you have righted wrong. You're a hero. And you're my great granddaughter." Samra croaked, his voice rather coarse. I gave a dazed smile. Then, I closed my eyes and fainted.

18. Welcome

"She's done so much, though no-one really knows what!" a vaguely familiar voice said, close by. I gave a start. I was lying on a bed, one that was completely white. There were other beds with children on, but they were hardly visible through the crowds of people that were staring at me.

"Jadie! Where did you go? I think I dozed off for a second and when I woke up, it was late in the night, and you had disappeared. Did you go to Mira's?" someone asked. I noticed that it was my mum. She winked at me. I gave a brief smile. I knew what she meant, and I wasn't sure how much she knew. Her face was covered in fingernail marks and there were black circles underneath her unusually bright eyes. I wrapped my arms around her and nodded.

"Mira's in the bed next to yours and so are Jake and Liam." My dad said, who was perched at the end of the bed. I gave a nod, Samra's face swimming in and out of my vision.

"Oh, Hi Miss Hills!" came a sweet voice. Up my nose, a scent of sweet honey and vanilla came. It made me feel dizzy, sleepy, and happy all at the same time. I gave a small smile. A bright, jolly looking nurse dressed in a spotless, unblemished apron came towards me, smiling as she patted down her apron, beaming at me. "We've never had such an exciting patient!! We had a phone call into our emergency lines giving us an address to collect you and the other children. It sounded like a man's voice, very hoarse and throaty," The nurse said, "but when we found you, there was no-one there! We were so intrigued! I know this sounds a bit funny dear, but do you know anyone with a hoarse, throaty voice?" she asked sincerely.

I tried to take in her appearance. She had chocolatey-brown skin and her pockets were filled with tools and instruments.

"No." I shook my head and tried not to smile.

"Very well…" the nurse kept on smiling but she looked slightly disappointed, "I'm terribly sorry… my name is Nurse Hazel and I'm in charge of the Children's Ward. Now, there are only four of you. There's Liam, Myra, and Jake?"

"No, it's Mira." I said, smiling slightly and chancing a glance at them. I couldn't help liking this nurse greatly. I now noticed that she had a tray, laden with my favourite types of food:

- A glass of hot chocolate
- A home-made pancake with a reasonable amount of syrup
- A bowl of melons, freshly cut

And many more tasty treats. As the nurse lay it on my knees. My grandmother was there, arguing with the nurse. She had brought her own selection of food: samosas; jamoons and many more delicious bits. Nurse Hazel suddenly gave up and the next thing I knew was my plate being topped up with more food. I wanted to bury my face in it, but instead chewed it slowly. After what seemed like 3 years, I had finished the mountain of food and now desperately wanted to see my friends. Jake had sat up and was grinning at me. I tried to smile back and get out of bed, but Nurse Hazel literally shoved me back in. She drew the curtains around my bed and insisted that I needed sleep and rest. My mum wanted to talk to me. "Please Nurse Hazel. It will help us all." she pleaded. Nurse Hazel who kept on smiling (though very falsely) reluctantly agreed to let her talk to me.

"Jadie, it is wonderful to see you alive and well, but you must tell me what happened. The lovely nurse won't let me keep you talking for more than 10 minutes."

I quickly told her the whole story, ignoring her gasps or hurried looks for the nurse. At the end, she stared at me, her eyes filled with tears and love.

"Well done, Jadie."

I smiled and gave her a hug. Then, Miss Hazel bustled in and told my mum to go. My mother gave me a kiss and went off saying, "See you in the morning!" I sniffed.

"And look now!" Nurse Hazel muttered with a slight scowl, "All that unnecessary talk isn't going to make her feel over the moon!"

She wished me good night and tucked me in. I rolled over to my left and went straight to sleep. Then, I felt myself being rolled to the right and saw three sets of eyes looking down at me. I let out a little yelp, which was hastily stifled by a large hand.

"Shut up, its us!" Jake's voice hissed. I sat up and almost leapt out of bed. Before I could, I was tackled into a giant bear hug. I could feel Mira's arms around me.

"Come on Jadie! Tell us what happened after we lost you when we tried to shadow travel. Jake and I got separated from you and Liam," Mira said, "just as I was trying to focus, I suddenly felt myself freeze and all I could see was a bright green light. I saw a green slimy thing covering me. I could see you and Nephia have a good old chat about the weather. At one point I swear I saw a snake. I think it was a python."

"Rattlesnake." I muttered.

"Well… it's a long story…" I told them everything. I tried to make it sound impressive, skimming through the bits where I felt like I was going to die. Liam was not helpful. He kept on interrupting me and being a nuisance. At the end, I gave a little yawn and told them all to go back to bed. Waving goodbye as if they were going on a holiday for 5 months, they slowly and reluctantly did.

I calmly closed my eyes. I dreamt of swimming in the deepest oceans, of climbing the highest mountains and achieving all I wanted to do.

As I slept, I realised how lucky I was to have had these adventures. How lucky to be me.

EPILOGUE

My name is Miss Jadie Hills. I run the Hotel SAMRA.

I have my room in the top floor and there is a museum at the side of the hotel. The main attraction is a rock with a glimmering emerald in the inside. There is a special floor (floor 5) which is accessible only to V.I.P members. There are only a few of them:

- Miss Mira Partail
- Mr Jake White
- Mr Liam West
- Mr Paul and Mrs Julie Hills
- Mrs Lucy Hills

The Hotel Samra has several fun activities for both children and adults. There is a special room – which is near the pool area, called - The Everdark room. This room itself is a small theme park, filled with different types of thrilling and scary rides.

The receptionist, who happens to be Miss Mira Partail, always hands out sweets to all children who come in. My parents stay here quite often, and Mr Jake White practically lives here. I find it incredibly difficult to keep up with the number of people who visit but they all love it.

As I walked up the balcony to watch the sunset one evening, I thought I saw a figure, dressed in a blue coat, with kindly eyes slipping into the water. I knew that my mind was playing tricks on me. But, as I turned away from the balcony, I felt the warm feeling that I had experienced several years ago. I smiled.

THE END

About the Author

Siona Rao is 10 years old and lives in Bristol, England with her parents and younger brother. She goes to St Michaels C of E Primary School in Stoke Gifford.

She has a great passion for reading and writing. Her all-time favourite book is the Harry Potter series. Siona draws inspiration from several authors and works very hard to create her own characters and plots. She hopes to engage readers with her imagination into the world of magic, created in a way that magic can strike anybody, and it can be good or evil.

Printed in Great Britain
by Amazon